DARREN PAUL MCKEEMAN

City of Apocrypha

First published by Barbary Coast Books 2000

Second edition

ISBN: 978-1-7371997-2-4

This book was professionally typeset on Reedsy.
Find out more at reedsy.com

To my firstborn child.

Contents

1

Prologue: Weirdness Magnet

There's a friend of mine who claims I'm a weirdness magnet. I suppose it's the fact that I always have a weird story to tell her whenever I call her. I told her about seeing heads skitter across the freeway during a nasty accident I once witnessed. I seem to have witnessed far more than my fair share of fatal accidents. I also told her about the time I was walking back to my hotel in New Orleans after spending a night on five hits of acid and Satan himself offered to blow me for $5 from the back of a long dark limousine.

Things seem to have calmed down since I moved to San Francisco, but I think that's because this city is so weird to begin with.

San Francisco has a long and fine tradition of being a weirdness magnet. Emperor Joshua Norton I may have started this tradition during the days of the Gold Rush. Joshua Norton was a merchant from South Africa in the 1850's. He had a master plan: controlling the rice market in San Francisco, which was very big due to the large number of Chinese immigrating to help build the railroad.

His plans went awry when he lost his entire fortune buying rice futures. A ship from China came in the very next week unexpectedly bearing a load of rice and he was totally wiped out. He did what any rational man would do in his situation. He went totally stark raving mad and crowned himself Emperor of the United States and Protector of Mexico.

It probably wouldn't have even been noticed if he hadn't notified the newspapers on a slow news day. The editor decided it would be good for a laugh and printed the Emperor Joshua Norton I's proclamation on the front page as straight news. A legend was born.

The good Emperor is responsible for a great many San Francisco traditions. His proclamations instituted the lighting of the Christmas tree in Union Square. He was the visionary behind the Bay Bridge to Oakland. He dissolved Congress and also made it illegal to call San Francisco 'Frisco', offenders to be fined the huge sum of twenty-five dollars.Well, it was big in those days. It's still a lot of money just for saying 'Frisco'.

The people of San Francisco loved Emperor Norton. He was allowed to print his own money and it was honored in most establishments in the city. Restaurants fought over having him eat in their places of business. Mark Twain based a character in Tom Sawyer on him. The Masons paid for his hotel bill. When he died, over 100,000 people attended his funeral.

It's almost like people have been trying to imitate him ever since. Take local politics, for instance. At a birthday party for a prominent city figure, a performance art piece involving a man calling himself the Satanic Apache Front had a woman carve a pentagram into his back and sodomize him with a whiskey bottle. Of course, it caused a scandal in the papers – but pretty much every person on the street thought it was very boring.Worse things happen in SOMA every night and mostly to people who pay to have it done to them.

The politicians in San Francisco, most of whom attended this party, all said the same thing to the newspapers. They all said, "We had left the party by the time that happened."

As the end of the millennium approached, this town was all about the politics of party-going.You had to deftly avoid scandal while being seen. It could be fun, especially when you came to the realization that in San Francisco the party for the end of the Millennium had already started and everything else was sort of secondary at that point.

These are things I have only read about. The actual people I've met are much stranger. I guess it's the weirdness magnet in me. Some people I've known for a while, like my friend John from Seattle. I'll tell you more about him some other time. Others I've only met recently, like Lloyd Stark.

I first met Lloyd while walking through Golden Gate Park. I was strolling there, and he was trying to get me to buy some low-grade smack he'd been selling to the hippies there. I ended up talking to Lloyd, and found out a great many things about him. I lied to him about what I did for a living, my name, and where I lived.

Of course, the real reason that I found Lloyd is that my weirdness magnetism attracted him to me.

Lloyd is a pretty interesting guy. I got his name and number that day in the park 'in case I wanted to buy anything'. He's also not a bad writer. He writes hardcore gay pornography to make a living, which is extremely funny considering that he's straight. He also receives a small stipend from a trust fund set up in his name. He doesn't talk about it much, but what little he has said about it seems to revolve around a doctor in Texas and black-market human organ transplants. When subjects like that come up, I tend to not ask too many questions.

Well, back to the politics of party-going. I recently had a party that ended very badly for me. I had been looking into the possibility of having a Halloween party, a holiday that I love very much. It also happens to be the birthday of my girlfriend, Cathy.Well, I had envisioned something grand and had wanted to rent a hall for it, but when time came around for it I found that the hall I had wanted (actually an abandoned church) was rented out to a movie crew that weekend.

I gave up and made plans to go to a friend's party. Well, I had been telling everyone around I was thinking about having a party. When I told them that my plans had fallen through and I was planning to attend another party, for some weird reason they assumed that I was going to be the host of this other party.

Well, it wasn't any normal group of people who decided this. This was a small group of speed freaks that used to live in this town. They have since disappeared, under mysterious circumstances. You see, I happened to bring Lloyd Stark to this party, and he saw everything that transpired that night.

Somehow, this group of people convinced the host of this party that I had conned him into having it as a birthday party for my girlfriend. The host then demanded that we clean his apartment before we left.

Well, Catherine cleaned the entire apartment and refused help from anyone. We could only sit by and idly get pissed (and Lloyd and I were already drunk) while watching these stupid speed freaks degrade my girlfriend.

Cathy urged me to forget it, and I tried. Lloyd, however, is a different matter.

The story, as I heard it, is that one day these speed freak kids had just scored a big meth rock and had settled into some dingy apartment to scrape powder off it and snort it. They sat around idly talking and they each cut themselves a line. The person who started snorting first just happened to be a girl named Roxanne. Roxanne was a trust fund baby from New York City, out here on grandma's money and sleeping with every club promoter in town, even the ones with girlfriends.

According to her ex-boyfriend (whom she still lived with), Roxanne inhaled deeply, looked up with a pained expression on her face, and sneezed blood and sinus tissue all over the wall. In less than fifteen seconds, the inside of her sinus cavity was eaten away by the bad meth, which had either accidentally or purposefully been made with a little too much of a certain type of acid used in making speed.

She didn't die, but from what I understand she probably wishes she had. Her sinuses are still being rebuilt and her deviated septum was replaced with a piece of surgical plastic. The chemicals soaking her brain damaged it and turned her into a drooling mess. I heard she retained enough intelligence to attempt suicide three or four times.

The only suspicion I have about what happened is from Lloyd's offhand comment to me a few days after it happened.

"It's a real shame what happened to that speed whore Roxanne, ain't it?" he said with a twinkle in his eye. I had found out that day.

"Yeah, it sure is. Someone's selling bad speed in this town, Lloyd."

"Yeah, they sure are."

"I thought you knew every speed dealer in this town."

4

Lloyd looked at me for a second and smiled. "Yeah, I sure do. And you'll never get a bad batch of speed, if that's what you're thinking."

"Thanks Lloyd. That's comforting to know, but I really don't do speed."

"Well, at any rate, I think it's just karma for ruining Cathy's birthday party," he said. Nothing else was said about the matter.

The whole town of San Francisco used to be about the politics of party-going. If you were going to have a good time, then you could do fine. If you were out to ruin someone else's good time, then there's no telling what would or could happen. Karma will bite you on the ass every time.

My weirdness magnet is still active.

2

The Beginning

It all starts with Catherine, of course.

I met Catherine in San Francisco about three years before what turned out to be the end of life as we know it on the planet Earth. We didn't know it, of course. You never know with something like that. There are some things in life that you know instantly, and that's the way it was with Cathy and me. The instant we met, we knew that we'd be together for the rest of our lives. One of us might die first, but we'd be together forever in spirit. It's cheesy stuff that greeting card companies write cards for.

From the very beginning, Cathy realized that she had competition for my affections. She used to joke about it. "I'm just a mistress," she'd say. "I take a backseat to San Francisco."

It was almost the truth. I fell madly in love with San Francisco while on contract to a large technology firm with a three-letter acronym for a name. It helped that they'd provided a rental car and free lodging in a hotel for close to nine months. I was amazed that the job had taken that long to peter out. I hardly spent any time working, but rather I drove around slack-jawed trying to comprehend what I was seeing. In the end, the only explanation I had was that I had found the place where I would die and some primordial part of my brain had recognized it for what it was.

I formed a pact with San Francisco in those early days. I always talked to it as if it were a living being, but only when I was alone or with people that understood my love affair. I stated it simply one day after a climb up Strawberry Hill in Golden Gate Park to view the distant skyline.

"I'll make you a deal," I said to the skyline. "If you promise to keep my life interesting, I'll always pay my taxes."

The city stared back at me. Mute, of course. The day after I said this, I met Catherine.

I met Catherine through a close mutual friend of ours named Samantha Strange. Word on the street was that Sam had steered Cathy towards me because we both liked ferrets. The truth is that I'd seen her around the neighborhood and had asked about her. Another truth is that she'd asked about me the week before. The approach to that first meeting was slow and sticky, much like the first six months of our relationship. We met in the local coffee shop, with Sam looking smug and obviously gloating. Sam hung around for about thirty minutes and then begged off. It turned out later that she was trying actively to get Cathy to dump someone. It didn't take much, as she found out.

I had become intrigued by the sight of Cathy stalking down the street, dressed in fishnets and combat boots. She was always wearing a skirt that was dangerous to bend over in, and soft black sweaters to ward off the chill that permeated the San Francisco summers. A pair of vintage cat-eye glasses perpetually dominated her face. One of the first things I asked her about was her choice in eyewear, and she told me about finding them in a secondhand store, and having the prescription changed to match hers. It has been said that I have a fetish for these eyeglasses. She hardly ever took them off, especially after she met me.

Cathy and I talked for close to three hours the first night, and made plans to meet again the next night. This turned into a silly little ritual that we continued even after we moved in together. We knew from the start that we'd met the person we were going to be spending the rest of our lives with, and it didn't really matter even if we got hit by a car the next day.

"See you tomorrow," I said.

"If we live that long," she replied.

###

I probably would never have had the adventures I did, were it not for Cathy. I knew that my life was inextricably linked to her. My future was not even in question. I knew this about two months after we met. The signs came one afternoon when we met in Buena Vista Park and wandered up to Corona Heights.

Corona Heights is a harsh outcropping of rock that overlooks the Castro section of San Francisco. It's part of the park, and has been a recreation area ever since San Francisco was founded. The view is tremendous, and it's visible from almost every part of the city. Around sunset the light plays tricks with your eyes, and you imagine all manner of things if you see it from far away. Up close, it's just a craggy finger of rock pointing into the sky.

Cathy and I talked about many things in the early days. One of the things that I never understood about her was her spirituality. I understood that people needed to believe in things, but I approached it from the position of a scientist. I was, after all, a computer contractor; my entire livelihood depended upon basic principles of physics. The many contradictions between Cathy and myself were apparent.

Cathy was the child of hippies. She believed in a mishmash of pagan religions that she couldn't exactly explain to me. I admired her because she was just trying to figure it all out in the context in which she was raised. She'd never received the education I had, because her parents didn't put much emphasis on public education. As a result, she wasn't good at math, and she wasn't really that great at English skills. The latter would drive me insane. I spent a lot of my time writing documentation for computer systems, and I was a 'grammar Nazi', according to my friends.

"Can you hand that to me?" she asked me breathlessly, pointing at a stick lying in the bushes near my feet. We'd hiked up to the top and she was about to do some kind of ceremony for the new moon.

"I can," I replied. "You'll have to ask me nicely to get me to do it."

She smiled at me, recognizing this game from the first conversation we'd had.

"Smart ass," she smirked. She pulled out an asthma inhaler and took a hit off of it. Sometimes, it seems to me that almost everyone in California is an asthmatic.

"I just think that through constant reminder you might get it right some day," I said.

"Just for that, I'll do it just to irritate you," she shot back.

So it went with my Cathy. We puttered around the summit, watching the sun sink lower.

"So why do you do this?" I asked.

"Do what?" asked Cathy.

"This ritual," I said.

"I'm trying to get more in touch with the cycles of the moon," she said.

"Why would you want to do that?" I asked.

"It was what our ancestors did," she said.

"Yeah, but they had a need to," I said. "We live in a city, there's not a real need to live by the seasons, or the phases of the moon, or things like that."

"Oh yeah?" she asked. "What do you think we should be doing?"

"Well, we don't really have a choice," I said. "We follow patterns and cycles that modern society has imposed upon us."

"How so?" she asked. She was pulling out a novena candle from her backpack and kneeling down in her fishnets and leather skirt. The candle was round, made of clear glass. It was colored red.

"Well, you should know this," I said. "You work at that store."

Cathy worked at a sex store in the south of Market, popularly called SOMA. Whether or not the nickname actually reminded people of a Brave New World was yet to be seen; it was fast turning into the center of multimedia and pushing the sex stores out at this time.

"I'm a retail whore, yes," she said. "And I first met you at that store."

"What?" I asked. I didn't remember this.

"Oh come on," she said. "You bought a corset from me."

The scene drew a blank, but I had bought a corset at that store. I couldn't remember my salesperson; it had been over a year ago.

"You don't remember me!" she squealed.

"Oh hush," I said. "I buy a lot of corsets."

"I'll remember that," she said. She went back to her novena candle, and pulled out some vials of sweet-smelling oil.

"At any rate, you know when people buy more stuff," I said.

"Yeah, right after payday," she said.

"Those are the cycles that our society follows," I said. "I think that's why people are kind of nutty now."

"What do you mean?" she asked.

"We've lived so long based on the seasons, or the phases of the moon," I said. "Women are particularly vulnerable to it, if you want to get sexist. In the past few centuries we've gotten away from it and we are turning into beings that live around the clock on artificial cycles. I think it's making our society a bit psychotic."

"So what I'm doing isn't weird to you?" she asked as she drizzled the oil on the open end of the candle.

"Not particularly," I said. "It's you trying to stay sane in the banality of this reality by trying to recapture the cycles our ancestors lived by. I app rove."

"But do you believe in it?" she asked.

"No, not really," I said. "That doesn't mean it's not right."

"You are a weird guy," she said. "Is there any religion you follow?"

"No real religion," I said. "If I were going to follow something, I'd have to make it up."

"What do you mean?" she asked.

"Well, religion always provided a way of dealing with forces beyond your control," I said.

"Yeah?" she said. "So don't you think those exist anymore?"

"Well, they do," I said. "Our needs are much different these days. We don't need good crops, we need a parking space. Instead of praying to the god of crops, we'd have to find out who to worship to get a good parking spot."

"That's a force beyond our control, all right," said Cathy. "You have a car?"

"No," I said. "But if I did, I'd need a parking spot and there are damn few of those in this town."

"Something you'd need a god's help for, that's for sure," she said, sprinkling some herbs on her candle.

She finished dressing her candle and lit it. The sun was almost down.

"There," she said. "Now, we wait."

"For what?" I asked.

"Just watch the sun go down and shut up," she said.

"Is that it?" I said.

"Shut up," she said, and grabbed me by the back of the head. Before I knew what was happening, She had shoved her tongue down my throat and I had experienced the best sunset I had ever seen since I came to San Francisco.

As I kissed her, a flash caught my eye. I looked up while kissing her. Two shooting stars tracked lazily across the sky and flashed out over the Pacific. Fireworks. I realized that for the first time in my life, I had seen a sign. I was suddenly filled with hope, and I let my eyes close.

###

Presently the sun went down.

"So, how many corsets do you own?" she asked as we descended the hill.

"About two," I admitted.

"Mind if I come over and try them on?" she asked with a mischievous grin.

"Not at all," I grinned. "I am not totally enamored of them anyway."

"You're going to buy more, aren't you?" she asked.

"Why?" I asked warily.

"Well, when we move in together, I can borrow them," she said.

"Why wait?" I asked.

"It's just the way I do things," she said.

Neither of us suspected that she would be borrowing my corsets within a couple of months, but that's how it turned out. In a way, she was the reason that everything happened the way it did. I never would have been looking for cheap housing, and all the things that came out of that scheme, if it hadn't been for her. Then again, I'm getting ahead of myself.

3

The Opening of the Golden Gate

It was from Lloyd Stark that I first heard about the gateway to Hell that waits to open in the rolling hills of San Francisco.

Lloyd defies description. He's a massive man who looks quite a bit like Allen Ginsberg did when he was young. A massive tousle of curly brown hair framing a bearded face hiding behind thick horn-rimmed glasses is about the best I can come up with. I listen to Lloyd with a grain of salt, because I met him at Golden Gate Park. I was taking a walk, and he was trying to sell low-grade heroin to the destitute gutter hippies that live there.

"Hey buddy, wanna score some smack?" he asked me.

"Fuck off, dirtbag," was the first sentence I ever said to Lloyd. This is ironic, because now Lloyd is one of the better friends I have here.

"Come on, man gimme a break. I just sell it, I don't do it," he said, as if that made it all better.

"I only smoke weed," I said. This was true. I smoke large amounts of marijuana. This has made people actually accuse me of being a closet flower child. They usually change their minds after I show them that my idea of a good time is to get really stoned and watch snuff films over and over again while giggling.

He threw a small bag of marijuana at me and told me to smoke up, then walked away.

I didn't see Lloyd again for two months.

The next time I saw Lloyd, he had a job as a repo man. As far as I know, that's what he does to this day. You have to be an absolute bastard to be a repo man. I recognized him because he came to take away a car that one of my roommates was delinquent on. I watched with amusement as my roommate argued with Lloyd about how she'd sent the money in and Lloyd smirked at her constantly.

"You're shit out of luck, babe. I might let you keep it if you blow me, but then again I might not," he said.

"Hey, aren't you that guy I saw selling smack to hippies in the park?" I piped up.

Lloyd looked me up and down and grunted.

"Lots of people sell smack to hippies in the park."

"Yeah, but you gave me good weed," I responded.

"You're still not getting the car for her," he said.

"I just need more weed," I said, and at that moment I think a friendship was born.

###

Lloyd and I got to know each other over coffee at the local café. Every neighborhood has one, a corner coffee shop where early risers come to grab their mochas before scuttling off to the bus. The local café here is called the Café Abir. I have never found out exactly what the name means, but that's not really important. What is important is to know that Lloyd and I started talking about government conspiracies while surrounded by ornamental hookahs and onion-shaped arches. I had just written a short story after hearing a San Francisco urban legend about ultra-high frequency sound generators on top on the US Government building in the Tenderloin driving everyone mad.

"Yeah, they experiment on us!" said Lloyd. "Those damned politicians and their dirty narco-dollars are out to control us all."

Clarification is needed – when Lloyd talks about narco-dollars. It's a reference to his belief that the government sells drugs and starts drug epidemics in order to get more tax dollars to fight drug epidemics. It makes sense, more than the conventional way the government is supposed to work. This is one of the multitude of theories Lloyd has. Read on.

"I am always looking for buried secrets, or rumors, or urban legends," I said to Lloyd. "I use them as parts of stories."

"Do you know about Emperor Norton?" asked Lloyd. I had, indeed, heard of Emperor Norton.

"Do you know about Anton LaVey's curses?" asked Lloyd. Lloyd claimed to be a Satanist when asked about religious matters, but most people I know who claimed to be Satanists also lied a lot, so I'm not sure about any of them. I also knew about Anton LaVey's curses on just about everything that was or wasn't nailed down in San Francisco. A lot of things pissed him off – he cursed a Safeway food store because they built it on a favorite park of his, and he cursed the Fox Plaza high-rise apartment tower because they'd destroyed the theatre where LaVey acted as organist in order to build the tower. The city is riddled with places cursed by the Church of Satan. It amuses me.

"Do you know about the Elder Sigil that will throw open the gates to hell at the turn of the millennium? That's obscure," he said.

"Say what?" I asked.

At this point, I have to explain what a sigil is, merely for those who do not know. It's a symbol or design that supposedly confers some sort of magic power. I used to watch an ex-girlfriend make them when she worked at a local magickal supply store.

"I didn't think you would have heard of that, it's mostly only known by locals," said Lloyd. The word 'local' stuck out at me and got under my skin. "It was designed by Aleister Crowley himself."

Now, I always get a little wary whenever anyone mentions the name 'Aleister Crowley'. Maybe it was the fact that the man was an accomplished and inveterate liar. Maybe it's the fact that when I read most of his books they come off as rather sexist. Or it just might be that I think he's in the same league as Marilyn Manson in that he claimed he was the Antichrist too, except he was a little more original about it.

"It's all in the statues.

"You see, back around the turn of the century, a group of devoted acolytes decided that since the turn of the millennium was coming, it might be a good idea to throw open the gates of Hell and spark Armageddon. They took a map of the San Francisco peninsula and decided that it would be an interesting thing to build a city-sized magickal sigil and perform rituals over it for 88 years.

"On their map," said Lloyd as he grabbed a napkin and pen and started drawing, "they plotted out a sigil as large as the entire city. They figured out where the ley lines and major nodal points of ley line power were in San Francisco. They used all of this to figure out the points where they could play connect the dots in the city, and tried to erect statues at each of the points on their map.

"They had a very hard time with downtown San Francisco, until 1906 and the big earthquake. With most of downtown demolished, they generously donated rebuilding money and erected statues anywhere they damn well pleased. Not bad for a bunch of rich sodomistic devil worshippers," said Lloyd.

I chuckled until Lloyd showed me the napkin. On it was a rough map of the peninsula, and ten dots on it. He had drawn between the outermost five and my blood ran sort of cold for a second. He had drawn a huge pentagram across San Francisco.

"Here's the addresses of the statues," he said. "Check it out."

###

I did check out Lloyd's story, and the more I delved into the strange mystery, the more it frightened me. Being the child of technology I am, I borrowed a portable GPS receiver a friend of mine had for laptop computers, and I visited each and every statue Lloyd had shown me. When I connected the dots by computer, the connecting lines between each of the outer five dots were exactly 2.3 miles long, and they were precise to within a foot or so. The inner dots were also precise to within a foot. That sort of thing really doesn't

15

happen by accident, and I suddenly was forced to consider that someone had actually done this on purpose. That having been proven sufficiently to myself, I also decided that the rest of the story might be true. Someone had built a giant pentagram in order to open the gates of Hell.

I don't believe in Hell.When people ask my religion, I say 'Zen Buddhist', safe in the knowledge that most people don't know what that is anyway. But with Judeo-Christian upbringing, I still felt a weird twinge when looking at my mapping software made by a huge software company that is headquartered somewhere outside Redmond, Washington.

Well, it's pretty creepy when you figure out something like that, especially if you're paranoid enough to maybe think that Microsoft may have had a hand in it just because their software showed me the proof.

This is all far from over, I remember thinking.

4

Bridge-Hopping

I t was a beautiful day in San Francisco. My friend John and I decided it would be fun to go to the Golden Gate Bridge. Besides, from what we knew, the number of people to take a header off the bridge was getting close to a thousand; maybe we'd get to see number one thousand take his or her place in history.

John was an unusual boy. His idea of funny sent most people screaming for the hills. This meshed neatly with my own worldview, in which I wanted people as far away as they could get. This is hard to accomplish in San Francisco. He was a raving paranoid who liked to fondle himself while talking. For this reason we all called him Crotchtoucher John. I mean, seriously – how many Johns do you know? I know about thirty. People know exactly who I'm talking about when I say Crotchtoucher John.

We took the bus to the San Francisco side of the Bridge. If you've never been to the Golden Gate Bridge, you should; it's a neat place. There's an old fort directly underneath the bridge, where toxic flecks of lead-based red paint rain continually. The Bridge itself has two suspension spans, with enormous cables ten feet in diameter lashing the roadway down. It's a miracle more people weren't killed building it. The water underneath churns angrily, because this is where the bay meets the angry expectations of the sea. There are old ships down there, but it is risky to excavate them because of the current and the great white sharks that prowl the coastline sometimes.

For these reasons, it's a pretty good place to kill yourself. The city government has had such a problem with this that they've installed telephones that go directly to the suicide hotline every ten feet along the bridge. It's in the best interest of the depressed person to seek help before they actually jump, because once they've hit the water they are pretty much as good as dead. It's well over a two-hundred-foot drop to the mouth of the bay, and impact is liable to break quite a few bones. Treading water in the vicious undertow would probably be impossible, even without broken limbs. This is the same violent current that makes it impossible to swim anywhere from Alcatraz Island. There's only one recorded case of anyone surviving a fall from the Golden Gate Bridge, and that was because the person who jumped hit the water ten feet away from a small sailboat which happened to be carrying a medical doctor trying to relax. I can't help but try to imagine this poor doctor's thoughts sometimes. "Gee, it sure is nice to be out of the hospital, not being responsible for anyone's life." Splash.

The coastline across the Bridge is gorgeous. It's a spot called the Marin Headlands. If you watch Star Trek, this is where Starfleet has its headquarters on Earth, and it's the one thing that makes me believe that Star Trek is a tool of Satan. Any civilization that advanced should not go around destroying large sections of historic unblemished coastline for a cool headquarters. If anyone actually proposed building a giant spaceport in the Headlands, I'm sure that California would probably revolt. The place is far too pretty to be developed – but all across the cliffs you can see evidence of the military control of this piece of beachfront property. World War II-era bunkers and anti-aircraft gun mount points betray the past. Hopefully they'll leave that all alone.

Crotchtoucher John and I spent the entire day crawling around in the labyrinth of tunnels that made up the bunker system. While we were at it, I asked him about the giant pentagram over San Francisco.

"Sounds a lot like the Zodiac Killer," said John.

It's funny how often weird stuff like that happens to me. Seemingly unrelated passions of mine develop strange synchronicities. In this case, John was right, and he started in on his knowledge of the Zodiac, which was much greater than my own. The Zodiac Killer had killed people in specific places to form a pattern across the Bay Area, a shape roughly like the letter Z. An attentive young man in recent years noticed that the Zodiac Killer's taunting letters to the police all had different postmarks. Highlighting where he sent the letters from on a map makes a giant pentagram across the Bay Area. Coincidence?

"There are no coincidences," said Crotchtoucher John, waving his flashlight around. Coincidentally, at this point in his rant he fell into a hole in the floor that was about four feet deep and filled with fetid black water. I had to rescue him. We decided to leave the tunnels before we broke our necks.

###

"John, I want to show you something," I said as we emerged sneezing into the bright California afternoon.

"More pentagram stuff?" he asked.

"Yeah, I guess so," I said. The Golden Gate Bridge had one of Lloyd Stark's Satanic statues sitting right in the parking lot.

"Well, bring it on," said John.

We walked down a small mountain road onto the sidewalk. We were on the Marin County side of the Golden Gate Bridge and had to walk across the bridge to get back to the bus stop. Juniper bushes, light brown dusty sand, and strange plants that looked like the jade trees my grandmother used to grow, lined the side of the small asphalt strip and dropped away from us as the sidewalk carried us onto the hulking steel platform. Glimpses of an angry Pacific Ocean between girders reminded us to stay on the sidewalk. Tourists by the dozens were hanging around, walking up and down and snapping pictures. I looked around and felt slightly irritated at everyone. John was muttering curses under his breath at the unwashed masses. Of course, we were being stared at. John had long purple and red extensions in his black hair, and this was right around the time I was walking around with my head shaved. Besides, we were soaking wet from the waist down, shivering, and dressed in black military garb we'd gotten at the local surplus store. The trenchcoats didn't help, either.

Sometimes I can feel my weirdness magnet kick in. As we walked across the bridge, a man appeared from the opposite side of the Bridge. He had a determined look on his round twentysomething face. He definitely was not a tourist, and I could feel my weirdness magnet (kerchunk) turn on as if at the end of a crane in a car crushing yard. My eyes met the eyes of the young man in front of me.

In retrospect, he was nothing special. He looked as though he might have been from a nice family, had a well-paying job in SOMA maybe. He definitely looked like he lived in SOMA, the multimedia boom area of San Francisco. He was wearing extremely large corduroy pants, about four sizes too large for him and a nasty dried-blood color. I remembered at the time thinking that at least his pants were the color of blood. His shirt had horizontal thin stripes across it in many different colors, all drab olive or greenish. His dirty blond hair swept across his head in a four-inch-long slash and he had piercing blue eyes

His eyes met mine for an instant, and I felt the smack of a carload of weirdness solidly slam into the surface of my magnet. A chill ran up my spine as we both stopped for a second. Then it was over, he had stumbled past me and I was hurrying to catch up to John, who had a fear of heights and wasn't coping well with his own morbid curious impulse to look over the side. He always wants to jump when he gets in a place with a long drop.

We curled around the steel girders marking the end of the Bridge and wandered into the parking lot with its magnificent view. As we moved among the throngs of tourists, I heard a shout from up on the bridge and saw a smear of blood-red corduroy streak downward from the Bridge. I had stared into the eyes of a suicidal man on my way across the Bridge, which is a haunting experience, to say the least.. We were in a place where the landing of the man in the water was totally obscured from us. Besides, I didn't want to see that.

It was when John cried out that things began to get truly weird.

"Shit!" shouted John.

"Yeah," I said, turning away from watching the crowd gather on the Bridge.

As I looked, I noticed John wasn't looking at the Bridge. He was looking at a tall imposing statue standing in a small garden next to a cross section of one of the cable bundles that held the Bridge up.

John backed up until his foot hit the edge of the sidewalk and he tumbled down into the dirt. He still scrabbled around, becoming more frantic as his eyes never left the statue.

"Dude, what's up?" I asked. I have a bad tendency to say the word 'Dude' a lot.

"Let's go, man!" John practically shouted at me, as he struggled to get up. I offered my hand and he hurriedly grabbed it, nearly pulling me down in his need to get up. I had to chase him across the parking lot.

As he stopped to catch his breath, John explained to me what had spooked him.

"That statue looked at me, man," stammered John. "I mean, it turned its head and LOOKED at me."

We got on the bus and didn't talk the entire way home. There was nothing on the evening news about the man who jumped from the Bridge. At John's insistence, I called my friend Natasha who worked at the San Francisco Examiner as a reporter. As I got off the phone, I told John what I had found out.

"The reason that it wasn't on the news was because that man was the nine hundred and ninety seventh person to jump from the Bridge," I told John.

John got very quiet, as did I.

"I think that whatever you told me about those statues," John said, "has something to do with this."

We sat in my room for a while as an ominous sense of dread filled both of us.

5

The Plan

I'd had 'The Plan' in my head for a while, but I never knew exactly how to make it come true. It should have been simple. Find several like-minded people and rent a large house in the giant neighborhood just north of Haight Street that most of our friends lived in. The problem was not in the idea, but in the execution. We had, perhaps, too many like-minded people interested in this plan. We all realized that we needed a lot of room, but the problem was that housing in San Francisco was extremely hard to break open all at once the way we needed it to.

We had, depending on the season, about twenty people interested in this plan. We almost thought about renting a twenty-room mansion in Pacific Heights, but we realized it would be too hard to explain. The problem was not that we lacked the people to do such a thing, but rather that there was just no housing.

I usually met my two housing conspirators for breakfast on Saturdays. Lloyd Stark claimed he needed the grease to survive, and made us go to his favorite café at the corner of Fulton and Divisadero. "Crotchtoucher" John Cooper met us there. I had my doubts about John as a roommate. I had never figured out where his money came from, but I knew that he was currently unemployed. One of my own personal requirements for a roommate was a job. As far as I knew, Lloyd had given up dealing heroin and become a repo man.

"I'll get a job!" said John. He gave me the creeps, yet I still hung around him. In retrospect, it wasn't such a good idea to have him around.

"Yeah, sure." said Lloyd, swigging coffee. "We'll give you until a month from now, then we stop counting on you."

I shot Lloyd a look, one of my looks that said 'Don't make a deal with John', when the door to the greasy spoon opened directly behind Lloyd. The place was small, about forty feet by forty feet with a jutting laminated counter against one wall. An elaborate mirror with trim buried under generations of paint, reflecting upon the shelves holding coffee mugs, lined the wall behind the counter. Five full booths and two half-booths were scattered around the floor with an amazing complement of condiments covered in the stickers of the neighborhood—Hello Kitty, photo-stickers of people, custom-made stickers advertising odd projects, local bands, and pure dada. Once again, Lloyd had ordered pancakes in hope of getting his favorite syrup container. He'd put a sticker on it to signify which one it was, but it seemed that the people next to us had gotten it. Lloyd hadn't noticed this yet. He had noticed the door opening behind him for some reason. I was going to chalk this up to coincidence when John sat up in his seat as well.

A man wearing a sweater striped with dark red and brown and faded blue jeans came into the diner. He had about an inch of thick brown hair all over the top of his head and he seemed to carry himself a little bit larger than he actually was. He practically swaggered into the diner. Not many people paid attention to him except for Helen, the woman who ran the place. She seemed to know him. I looked at Lloyd at the same time that he looked at me.

"Who is that?" I asked.

"I was just about to ask you that." said Lloyd.

"He's got to live in the neighborhood if Helen knows him."

"Let's ask Helen," I said, and I waved as Lloyd drained his cup—the latter a sure way to get Helen's attention.

###

I am an inherently nosy person. I admit this. I have a perverse desire to figure out what is going on around me. I fully blame the following misadventures on exactly that strange quality embedded in my persona. The fact that it went on for most of the year leading up to the end of the millennium is, most assuredly, a complete and total coincidence.

I am warning you here and now that if you ask me anything about the events I am about to describe, I will disavow all knowledge of them and deny that they ever happened. This is all fiction. Of course, the problem with this is that most of the events I am about to describe could potentially happen. Nobody misses the people who died. In most cases, they had taken great pains to erase their own pasts for reasons only known to themselves. I maintain a large enough profile and enough friends around that would just barely notice I was gone—just as a safety mechanism. I don't trust most human beings very much, but I do like who I am, for the most part. I have a bad tendency to be perfectly neutral toward what is going on around me, more interested in watching stories unfold. I see no reason to disturb the poor souls that are all figments of my imagination. That's what I'll tell you if you ask me, at least.

From Helen, we learned that the man lived 'up the street'. She didn't know anything past that, and the fact that he had been coming in about once a month for the past twelve years. She recognized him, but that was because she had a thing for faces. In short, about the only thing we learned was that he had lived somewhere in the area for close to twelve years.

"He never told me his name.," said Helen. "Some people are like that."

We all nodded in agreement.

The general consensus at the table was that we had learned all we were going to learn about this man, and we prepared to turn our attention back to the lists of apartments we had purchased from three separate apartment rental agencies in order to get our rental fees back. We ate our meals slowly and deliberated over the six- and seven- bedroom houses. We had our cups refilled several times to brace us for the rude afternoon ahead visiting the three overpriced Victorians we found. I was convinced that nobody in his or her right mind would rent to us, even though we had scraped together the first and last month's rent, plus a deposit. We all looked too scary. The argument against this was the fact that we actually did live in San Francisco. Maybe the landlords here were used to scary people. I had some adjusting to do.

We had paid and were thinking about leaving an hour later when a police car went by. As it got to the restaurant, the lights started up.

"What's happening, Derwood?" said Lloyd. He knew I hated that name, and had gotten everyone to use it. "Do you have your walkie-talkie thing on you?"

Lloyd was referring to a police band scanner I carried around. I had a friend who showed me the frequencies of the police bands in San Francisco, and from him I found out that by listening to 460.075 megahertz on the police scanner, we were listening to a channel that the police had designated "PIC-4", or Police Information Channel Four. This channel covered roughly the neighborhood we were in at the moment, the Western Addition and the Haight.

"Yes," I said as I pulled out the scanner. I didn't bother to correct Lloyd, mostly because I wasn't sure he'd had enough coffee yet to be in the mood to be corrected. I pressed a rubberized button on the thing to turn it on, and the front glowed as it squawked into life.

I dialed into police information channel four just in time to hear an address being read. Then the command came to move it to PIC-11.

In San Francisco, there are twelve channels that cover the entire city. They operate from powerful repeaters that are designed to stay working with very basic, common equipment. The reason for this is to facilitate communications during a disaster. Some channels have been subverted to other uses in recent times. One of these is PIC-11. This is the channel that special operations use. Evidently, the police officer was being put into direct contact with a specialist concerning this call.

I flicked the switch over until the frequency for PIC-11 showed up. I heard the distinctive squawk of wildly distorted data tones and I frowned.

"What the hell is that?" asked Lloyd.

"It's encrypted," I said, as I laughed.

"Why are you laughing?" said John.

"Because the police can be such idiots sometimes," I said, wiping a tear away. "They gave the address before they encrypted anything."

"Fuckin' A," said Lloyd. "Did you get it?"

John spoke up. "I did, it's up the street."

###

We went to the address recited on the police band. It was actually a narrow alley between two ominous Victorians, with the normally locked gate open and police pouring in and out of it. It seemed extremely odd, and we could find out nothing more than the fact that a coroner's van showed up. Once again, the government had thwarted our plans to get a good look at gruesome stuff.

As had happened in the diner, all three of us noticed the man in the rusty red sweater walking along the street, walking through the police officers and waving hello to at least one of them. The officers grimly went about their business. Suddenly, our interest level went through the roof.

"Curiosity killed the cat," I said as I started down the street.

"We ain't cats," said Lloyd.

"This is weird," said John.

We followed the man, who didn't look back, until he reached a slightly worn Victorian, painted a nasty pastel green color, about a block away from the panhandle extension of Golden Gate Park on Page Street. We followed him for thirteen blocks, coincidentally. I understand a little bit more of what that is all about now. The house was in a residential neighborhood and children played in the streets as a group of people stood on a house's porch across the street. People were enjoying a spring afternoon in the neighborhood. I broke away from Lloyd and John, walking across the street to their hissing protests.

I reached him as he was walking into the alleyway next to his house. I spoke to him. I don't remember exactly what I said to him, because I touched him on the shoulder and my hand came away crimson slick. I looked straight into his eyes at that moment, and I saw him for what he really was—then the moment was gone, and he smiled at me. The air was thick with the scent of what must have been his cheap cologne.

"Would you like to come in and wash that?"

"Excuse me?" I asked. I looked back at Lloyd and John who were staring anxiously across the street at me.

"No, I don't suppose you would," he grinned.

"Who are you?" I asked.

"None of your business," he said in a slightly menacing tone.

"Does anyone live in the main part of the house?" I said, suddenly feeling the need to change the subject.

"No," the man said, looking angrily at me.

"No, I suppose not," I said.

The man looked at me oddly. I looked at my hand again. Lloyd and John stayed across the street, looking rather worried.

"Why not?" I asked.

"Because I want some privacy," the man hissed at me.

"Did you think about sealing the door that connects the downstairs and the upstairs?" I asked cheerfully.

"Go away!" the man hissed. He clearly looked unhappy.

"Aha!" I said. "Let's not mince words here, sir. I know something is up. I'm not sure exactly what, but it's suspicious enough for me to call the police—and I have a sample of blood on my hand right here."

"You couldn't possibly be blackmailing me, could you?" His tone had changed suddenly, to one of outright revulsion. I could tell what was happening. He sensed a total loss of control over the situation and he was getting pissed about it.

I smiled quietly.

In the end, I had secured the top half of the house for my experiment in social planning. It had seven rooms in it. We asked nothing of our landlord save that the door to the downstairs be sealed shut permanently. We would never set foot in the basement, nor would we ever ask to. We respected our landlord's privacy thoroughly. We also promised to pay him only in cash, and we pushed that through the mail slot in the downstairs door. In return for letting us rent the entire house from him (I offered him market rates and tried to make it a win-win situation for him) for the paltry sum of three thousand dollars per month, we would respect his privacy and not mention the blood-soaked sweater ever again. I attached a rider to this verbal contract—specifically stating that this privacy would be null and void if he ever turned on one of us.

Looking back on it, I realize that it might not have been the completely right thing to do. Unfortunately, the rental market in San Francisco sometimes requires that you overlook trivial things like having a serial killer for a landlord.

6

The Move-In

The rental market being what it is, it took us twenty-four hours to find a roommate. We had an arrangement with the landlord that nobody else would know what he was except for us three. I sort of broke that agreement with Cathy. At this point, Cathy and I had moved in together and were trying to save up enough to buy a house. This was no mean feat in San Francisco, and sometimes, heroic sacrifices had to be made in the interest of the common good. I had to tell Cathy everything I knew about our new landlord and hope she wouldn't freak out.

"Cool," she said.

I knew that this was pretty inappropriate for her to be saying, but I didn't say anything. Instead, what I did get was a tirade.

"Are you telling me this guy lives in the middle of a major center of population and he's our new landlord?"

"Well, yes."

"And you touched his shoulder and he was soaked in blood?"

"Again, yes."

"Do you think he might have been a butcher down at that butcher shop?"

"No, they wear big aprons," I said.

"And the police haven't caught him? Are they that stupid?"

"Well, I guess..." I didn't know what to say to this.

"And these people are too stupid to get away from him?" she demanded.

"Well, hon, I have the feeling that if Lloyd and John hadn't been there…"

"No, he was being stupid and trying to get caught and you caught him," said Cathy.

I considered this for a moment.

"How much is rent?" she asked.

"Excuse me?" I could scarcely believe my ears.

"This is San Francisco, it's hard to find a good deal on housing," she said. "Besides, if we get another roommate I'd be more worried about them."

"Really?" I asked.

"I can take care of myself," she said. As if to prove her point, she walked over to a rack on the wall and pulled down a KGB-issue nightstick, a layer of rubber around a piece of rebar steel. She smiled at me and handed me the hefty implement of destruction.

"It's fully five hundred dollars less than anywhere else for over twice the space anywhere else," she said. "I know people who would kill for something like that. I personally think that until I see it with my own eyes, I think that you have one hell of an imagination."

I never expected her to tell me that she loved me despite the fact that I was a notorious liar. I guess it was just back to me and Lloyd and John knowing about the serial killer in the basement.

###

We had two other roommates to get, and we got them both through people that we knew. One of them was Samantha, the door girl at one of the myriad goth clubs around town. We picked Samantha for many different reasons. Number one, we all agreed that it'd be neat to be able to get into the goth club for free. Number two, and more importantly, Samantha had a thriving business on the side as Mistress Lilith of *www.necromantic.com*. She was much the same as we were. Struggling and admitting it. She wasn't above letting us leech off her bandwidth—her personal teleconferences required her to have a fast connection. We helped her out with the bill and technical services, as I was working as a systems admin at the time.We knew she'd been looking for a place for a while, so we called her straight up.

We asked her what her favorite foods were.

"I'm a carnivore. I eat veggies sometimes."

We asked her what her favorite books were.

"I don't have time to read right now."

How often would she want to interact with us?

"I'll probably stay shut in my room most of the time."

We had all agreed to leave Sam in the dark about the landlord.

###

We interviewed two people the next day. They came from the local roommate referral place. We had given them our number about a week ago when Lloyd suddenly felt like he had to throw some chaos into the mix. He succeeded in doing this, but not in any permanent way.

The first person we interviewed was a young man who had just graduated from MIT. I got along with him well enough, but Lloyd dismissed him as 'too weird'. He'd never had a single drink of alcohol in his entire life. He was moving out here to San Francisco because he'd gotten a job with a software company throwing money around like it was some kind of rock star. I was familiar with the story. It made Lloyd's flesh crawl.

"I have a huge collection of digital images of porn drawn by people in the style of Disney animation," he said.

The second person we interviewed was a little closer to the mark, but we decided against him because he was a bicycle messenger. He had bright fire-engine red hair and took his bike everywhere with him. He was all kinds of punk rock too. Unfortunately, he was probably in diapers when real punk rockers first washed ashore here.

I listened to him drone on, gesticulating wildly to make some point that he never actually came to. In the end, I made myself firmly resolve to try to make some better excuse to everyone than 'I can't live with someone who has an Offspring sticker on their bicycle'.

I must now take a paragraph to explain to people from future generations who might read this story and wonder what in the hell an 'Offspring sticker' is. I will tell you that it is a piece of sticky paper on one side and the logo of a band that is currently being listened to. I know that I have just dated this entire story by explaining this, but if I'm gonna do it, I might as well go whole hog. I personally loathe this band, mostly because they covered a song by the Damned. I won't go into this here. Let's just say the subject is drama with me, OK?

"I like to think that I'm a pretty free-thinking individual. I mean, I'd be willing to live with people like you," he said.

"Like who?" asked John.

"Um, like you," he said. "I mean, you're all into that wearing black thing."

"I'm a Satanist," said Lloyd. The guy squirmed visibly.

In the end, things were awkward from then on with him. After he left, we all agreed that he didn't really fit in. To interview one more person from the agency would be torture. We gave up.

###

For the time being, we decided to keep it to just ourselves. We realized that we would be setting ourselves up for all kinds of weirdness. We had room for two more people in the house. We moved in on the first of February of 1999, and the instant we walked over the threshold with the first armload of stuff, John proclaimed that this would be a year-long party. I shot an evil glance at him and then went to check out the door to the basement.

The man had been true to his word. We'd gotten the keys in the mail and he wrote that he'd totally removed any connection from the top to the bottom part of the house. There was no visible place that made sense where you could go down. I knew logically where it should have been, but I could detect no trace of it.

"Wow," I said out loud.

We inspected the kitchen. Everything was covered with a thick layer of dust. The kitchen was large, and had antique cabinetry installed in it. All it needed was a good cleaning.

We spent the better part of that weekend cleaning. I was tempted several times to just take a hose and spray everything out, but I settled for a large mop and an industrial bucket with a mop wringer John had stolen from God knows where. Everyone claimed their rooms. Cathy and I claimed the rooms overlooking the street and to the side. They were connected via a closet, and one of them had been a library at one time. The bookshelves lined the walls.

Lloyd picked the uppermost room in the house. Most of the Victorian houses in San Francisco have a single tower-like feature on the opposite corner from the front door when you face them from the street. The top floor usually has a room with the conical cap of this tower, and this was where Lloyd wished to live. He spent almost no time cleaning it out, except to sweep it out and lug a few things to the top floor to sleep on. He started moving things in later on in the week.

John's room was on the second floor, the same as ours. There were three floors without the basement, and the top two floors were all bedrooms. The first floor was the living room, parlor, dining room and kitchen. There was a small porch out back with a washer and dryer, in obvious disuse, yet with no dirt on them. The backyard was immaculately kept, with a small Japanese rock garden and pond underneath a willow tree near the back and a yard leading to the backdoor of the basement. The grass looked like sod. John's window looked out upon this pastoral scene. I wondered what was under the sod as I watched him clean the room.

Sam took the one of the rooms upstairs across from Lloyd. There were three rooms on the top floor and four rooms on the second floor. We had the telephone company install a data line and split the cost between us, and we connected our respective computers to the internet. The process of moving in took about a month to complete, and in the meantime John's deadline to get a job was closing in on him.

The first night we spent in the house, Lloyd called me up to his room. We went into one of the rear rooms on the top floor, the one that Samantha hadn't moved into. From here, we climbed out onto the fire escape and up to the roof. We had a stunning view of San Francisco from up there. Then

Lloyd tugged on my shirt and pointed at the statue across from the DMV building, a block away from us in the Panhandle Park.

"Those damn statues are everywhere, man."

7

Smoke and Mirrors

"OK, I have a question," said John, as he handed a joint of something he called 'Mod Squad 2K' over to me. "You touched the guy on the shoulder, and your hand came away bloody?"

"Right," I said, inhaling deeply. I held it there.

"OK, so he was out in the open, soaked in blood, and nobody figured it out?"

John was starting to make a little more sense.

"Yeah," I said. "Isn't that kind of odd?"

"I'll say," said John. "I mean, even if he washed his hands, maybe some got on his jeans?"

"You're right."

"So how is just his shirt," said John "soaking wet with blood."

We were referring, of course, to our new-found landlord. Our landlord was quite insane, I had surmised. For one thing, the entire top portion of the house we now lived in looked to be rather unused since approximately 1979. The last people to inhabit the house had had a penchant for fuzzy blood-red wallpaper and swag lamps, but there was none of that in the kitchen where John, Lloyd and I held our Sunday morning conferences over a joint, brunch food, and Bloody Marys.

"How the hell should I know?" I asked no one in particular. "I touched him, his shirt was soaked with blood."

"Maybe the question shouldn't be how his shirt was soaked with blood," said Lloyd mysteriously, "but why..."

"Maybe the question should be 'What the fuck!' too, Lloyd," I spat.

"Yeah, really," he said.

"I'm just trying to figure this out," said John. "If he soaked the shirt in blood and then put it on, he'd have to clean his face and hands off. And then there's the problem of his blue jeans. Why wasn't it dripping down into his blue jeans?"

"I don't know!" I said, exasperated once again. "I just touched him and my hand came away bloody! You saw it!"

"I know, I'm just trying to figure out how he did this," said John.

"Maybe he painted it on with a brush after he killed that person," said Lloyd.

"He might have missed a spot in the back," said John.

"Maybe he has a friend," said Lloyd.

"No way!" said John.

Samantha came walking into the kitchen. We looked at each other.

It was enough to say that we noticed when Samantha came into the room. Normally, we saw her at the door to the goth club, taking money, directing people to the stamp guy, telling people they were not, in fact, on the list and had to pay like everyone else. Usually when she did this, she was in some exquisite latex or vinyl shiny outfit, looking like she'd kick your ass and make you like it. Right now, however, Samantha was dressed in a set of light pink pajamas with some large fuzzy slippers that looked like some kind of bat-like creatures on her feet, last night's makeup lightly smeared around her face, gone for the most part but not steamed off in the shower yet.

"Whatcha talking about?" said Samantha as she filled the teakettle from the tap. Going through the motions, not really comprehending what she was doing; it was kind of interesting to watch Samantha on autopilot for once.

"How about this, Samantha?" asked John. "Suppose you wanted to walk around wearing a shirt soaked in blood."

Samantha considered John out of the corner of an eyeliner-crusted eye.

"You serious?" she asked.

"Yeah," said John. "Except you had to do it where nobody would notice you."

"That's weird," she said.

"Yeah, it is," said John.

"I'd have someone else brush it all over me," she said.

"Yeah, but..." started John.

"I think it's too early for you weirdos," said Samantha.

"Heh, you always say that when I show up at the club at 9PM sharp too, Sam," said Lloyd.

"You're a unique case, Lloyd," said Samantha.

"But what if you had to do it by yourself?" said John.

"Weirdo," said Samantha. She snatched the joint from Lloyd's hand. It was about half gone.

"I wouldn't want to do it anyways," she said. "The smell would be atrocious."

"The smell?" I asked. I thought furiously. I hadn't noticed any smell. Why not?

"The smell of human blood is pretty distinctive," she said.

She took a drag off the joint and handed it to me, then walked to the sink.

"Have you smelled some of the people in our neighborhood?" I asked. "What person that grew up in the city knows the smell of blood?"

She looked like she considered it a moment. "You could be right, but there's too much of a chance that someone would notice it."

"That's the thrill of it!" said John, suddenly excited.

"What?" said Samantha.

"That's why he does it! For the thrill of almost being caught by a smart person!" said John, a little more enthusiastically.

"Uh, yeah," said Samantha, putting a dish in the dish rack.

"Um, we're working on a movie script, Samantha," I said.

"You and fifty million other people, "said Samantha, and she pulled out a bag of chips.

John shot me a look, and I shot him one back. Samantha didn't notice this; she was busy gathering herself up to leave the kitchen.

"Where's Cathy?" she asked.

"Out doing the retail whore thing," I said.

"Damn," she said. "I wanted to go down to the Haight later. Oh well. You guys talk to me when you get your script finished. I know this guy in Hollywood, he calls me up and watches my page."

Sam sashayed out the kitchen door, leaving us to contemplate her words.

"Yeah, okay," I said, noting her information for when I actually did write a script.

\###

I pulled down a mixing bowl after Samantha was gone. I was hungry, and I was going to make some pancakes. Lloyd and John didn't stop me, and they continued to talk while I sifted, mixed and whipped up a bunch of pancake batter. Thus came the origins of the Sunday morning Morbid Brunch. At first it was nothing but Lloyd and John and me, sitting around talking about our landlord. In truth, the roots lie in our mornings spent at Eddy's Café, trying to find a place to live together. We enjoyed each other's company far too much to stop eating together. It was sitting in the kitchen, week after week, reviewing what had happened to us the previous week, that made me decide to pursue the mysteries of San Francisco even more.

\###

"This shit doesn't surprise me," said Lloyd. "I've heard of too many fucked-up things in my time, man."

"What do you mean?" I asked.

"This city," he said. "There's something evil about it."

"No way," said John. "Cities aren't evil—they just are. People are evil."

"There's no way you can tell me that this place doesn't make people a little nutty," Lloyd said.

"That's because of the oppression of the government," said John.

"I thought you were a Nazi," said Lloyd.

"I'm not, I'm a socialist," said John.

"Same thing," said Lloyd.

"Not exactly. I realize that government is a necessary evil, and that the world must be polarized into two classes. There should be a small government class and a non-government class. The government class must decide what is for the common good.

"Wow, you're so Hitler," said Lloyd.

"So what, you're a Satanist," shot back John.

"I'm not arguing with you," said Lloyd. "Right on, brother."

I made pancakes, watching my two roommates banter about odd things and stupid dreams they'd never realize. It's one thing to have an army and to talk of political aspirations. It's another to be living above a serial killer and having proof of that knowledge. I made a note to myself that if it ever came to a point where I had to sacrifice myself for the greater good to protect the world from Lloyd or John, I would unhesitatingly do it. Just please don't let us lose the house.

8

Cadaver Tank

Y ou know how you were always bugging me to get a job?" asked
John.

"Yeah, I know," I said, grimly wondering what was up. I had
known John for right around two years and his job history was not good.

"I got a job," said John.

"Doing what?" I asked. The thought of John with a job actually terrified
me. He was a good strapping young man, quite strong in the back and suited
to just about any kind of work except actual thinking. He had the body of a
dancer and the hair extensions of Satan, at the moment.

"Down at UCSF," said John, and then he took a swallow from a paper coffee
cup he carried around. Ever since we moved into the house, I had noticed
that John didn't sleep very well.

"That's an improvement over Toys 'R' Us," I said, referring to the amazing
failure of working at the haunted Toys 'R' Us in Hillsdale.

John had a strange obsession with working in morbid places. It was like
he invited getting scared shitless. He invariably did. One such time was
working at the haunted Toys R' Us in Hillsdale. It was reputed to be haunted
by the ghost of an old woman who ran a farm on the property some one
hundred years ago. John found this out, and applied to work there, then
bragged about it for a week. The Tuesday after he started working there, he
came home from work one night and didn't leave his room for forty-eight

hours. When he finally did emerge, he never said a word about the job and would sometimes flinch if you said something about it. I studied his face for a reaction.

"Yes, quite a step up," he said. "But at least this place isn't actually haunted."

"What do you mean, 'actually'?" I said. "You're talking as if there's some doubt to the whole thing."

"Well, it's pretty creepy," he said. I groaned inwardly.

"What is it?"

"In the middle of the basement in the oldest building on the campus, there's a giant copper vat. It's a big round cylinder that has a few scratches and an amazing shiny finish. It's pretty well kept up by the staff, I mean they have the cleaning crew come down and polish it with Brasso every week. There's a porthole built into the side of it, and you can see through into this murky haze of souplike things that are a deep, rusty mud red.

"It's the cadaver tank," he said.

"The what?" I said.

"The cadaver tank. I am the person in charge of cataloging the body parts."

"Really?" I asked. "That's rad."

"Yeah," he said, getting into it. "That's the part of the medical center that is a college, and they do student dissections there. After each quarter, they would take the cadaver parts, eyes, skin, torsos, legs, arms, heads and everything and throw them into this vat. It's full of formaldehyde, you see? They have never ever emptied it. They can't, literally. To tow away that much formaldehyde is some kind of violation of an ordinance somewhere in the city's lawbooks, and they have to keep it where it is."

"No way," I said. The whole thing sounded doubtful to me. I was sure that maybe he'd gotten a weird job like that, but no way would a huge tank of formaldehyde be trapped on the peninsula like that. John had a tendency to lie to make things seem more morbid than they already were.

"You'll see," he said. "I will take you to work with me."

###

I must admit that going to see a huge tank full of cadavers and formaldehyde made me rather excited. I don't know what it is. My mother took a job at UCSF Medical Center at one point, and she never mentioned it to me. This made me curious. Was it something that nobody really talked about?

UCSF Medical Center is situated primarily on thirteen acres of land on a hill overlooking Golden Gate Park. It was built in 1898. The land was donated by Adolph Sutro, the former mayor of San Francisco. I'd seen the name before, in my research about San Francisco. One of the statues I'd visited was in a public park on the edge of the city by the sea, and I'd read a plaque that said it used to be Adolph Sutro's mansion and grounds.

Much as Emperor Norton I was an integral part of San Francisco, so was Adolph Sutro. He'd done a lot for the city. He'd come the year after the 1849 gold rush to be a tobacconist. He found himself slowly getting into banking, because the miners would come to his shop to buy tobacco and want to trade gold dust for it. He didn't want to be a banker, so he left his brother in charge. He made his fortune in 1860 when he invested in the Comstock Lode in Nevada. During that time, he ran afoul of 'The Octopus', as the locals called it—the railroad monopolies of the Southern Pacific Railroad.

When he came back to San Francisco, he found that he'd made a double fortune—his brother had opened the Sutro & Co. Gold Dust Exchange, and he was now not just enormously wealthy, he was stupidly wealthy. I admired the man when I read more about him—he used his fortune to build a streetcar line out to his house and grounds, which he'd turned into a public park. He also built a huge beautiful bathhouse by the sea, and it quickly filled with swimmers for the huge pools. Of course, he still made money at all this—5 cents a person for the streetcar line he built. This infuriated the Octopus—they wanted the job of providing public transportation to the prosperous and growing city. The problem was that Adolph Sutro was well loved by San Francisco, and at one point he owned over one-twelfth of the entire city. He was an eccentric millionaire who delighted in snubbing authority. If I had the money to do what he did, I would have done the exact same thing. Of course, today we have the government-run MUNI system. The running joke in the house was "Just when you think it can't get any worse, then MUNI gets there."

Nobody talks much about Adolph Sutro anymore, the same way nobody talks much about the cadaver tank. I think that's pretty sad, as he was a colorful old goat. I found my head full of images I'd seen in the library of old Adolph. He ran for mayor on the 'Anti-Octopus' ticket, and won handily. He died the year that the medical center was built, on August 8th, 1898. I'll always remember one photo of him in profile, with large white whiskers sweeping away from his well-manicured mustache and shaved chin. He looks like a ship's captain, only without the hat to conceal his receding hairline. He is indeed the Captain of San Francisco—he is the reason that the jutting oceanside portions of San Francisco look and exist the way that they do today. He built most of Golden Gate Park, building two enormous windmills that pumped water to irrigate the parched sand dunes of the western part of the city. After reading his history, it didn't surprise me to learn that he might have been involved in something as odd as building a giant pentacle across the young city of San Francisco.

We took the 6 Parnassus line from Haight Street on up to the Medical Center. It wasn't a far walk, but we didn't really feel like dealing with walking through the Haight, not in the morning. I would prefer to watch junkies being pulled from their apartments by coroners from the safety of a bus window. If I made that trip on foot, I'd never get anything done.

We got off the bus in front of an enormous Plexiglas display that scaled the side of the building, holding the working remnants of the first clock on that location. We walked down the street to a building that looked very, very old. Ivy-covered brick always makes me nervous in this city—it weakens the bricks by digging into them for purchase on its upward climb, and makes them that much more likely to fall over in an earthquake.

We entered into a door in the side of this building marked 'Employees Only'. We were immediately confronted by a stout Chinese man in a guard uniform. I was reminded of some villain in a James Bond film, the kind of guy who would take off his shoe and it would have a heel that turned into a razor-sharp boomerang or something goofy like that.

John signed me in, and then looked up. "This is the guy I was telling you about, Sam. The writer guy."

The guard frowned a second, and then did something unexpected. His eyes lighted up.

"Ah, the writer! Nice to meet you!" he said, pumping my hand vigorously up and down.

"Hi," I said nervously.Well, I did write, but it was mostly stupid things I shared with friends. I decided that the quiet observational bookish weirdo would be a good mask to slip into for this, and completely legitimate on my part.

"Dr. Morgan will tell you about any concerns we have about the facility," he said. "He's been waiting for you."

"Excuse me?" I said.

"Oh, I didn't tell him, Sam. Dr. Morgan wants to tell you some things and then he'll let you go into the facility," said John. I suddenly was frightened. I'd never heard John assimilate into a conspiracy so quickly. He was even starting to sound like them.

"Okay," I stammered.

We walked through the door and John suddenly was himself again. There was something else in the corridor with us. Faint, yet distinguishable from everything else. It was the smell of formaldehyde.

"Dude, just chill. I'm going to get you into this place, but I had to tell some stories to get you a little pass here. Nobody is supposed to know about this thing; they have to make sure that nobody in charge actually finds out about it. These guys are guerrillas, dude. They have a system that they've stuck to for years and years, and they aren't letting the government tell them what to do with it."

Suddenly, I saw how they had pitched the job to work with a totally carcinogenic substance to some young kid who didn't know any better. It made me a little mad at the time, but I don't care now. The tank doesn't exist anymore—that's a whole story unto itself. I'll get to it, don't worry.

We walked along an anonymous hall, filled with large steel doors that had hefty antique opening bars on them. A few of them actually had tooth and gear mechanisms attached to a giant twirling cross in the middle of the door.

I wondered what they stored down here that needed that sort of protection. Our shoes made tapping sounds that echoed in the long, dark corridor.

"This is my job," he said. "I am in charge of cataloguing the body parts. The students at the medical center dissect cadavers. They used to do it by the hundreds and this tank took only truly interesting specimens-the rest were cremated immediately. Now, they catalogue the parts, hold them in the tank, and cremate them in a facility a long ways from here. I write down what parts I find, make sure they all add up to X number of bodies, then I send them off every week when I fish them out of the tank."

We walked along the hallway past a few more doors, John explaining as we walked.

"They don't do as many dissections now. They don't have a morgue available for medical cadavers—they have too many dead people that need to be identified. It is most economical to hold the bodies like this and then cremate them in a week."

"They're cremating them after they've been treated with formaldehyde?" I asked. It was slowly sinking in what they were doing here, and why it was secret. "What if everyone did that?"

"Then we'd all be fucked," he said.

John stopped.

"They pay me pretty good," said John. "Maybe we should tell them about the serial killer, too?"

I stopped.

"You know," I said, "this is starting to feel like a very bad allegory where we make all the wrong choices."

###

Thinking about it, I spoke the truth to John there in the tunnel that day. I didn't make the wrong choice, though. I chose my friend. I knew that John was never going to be able to get a better job than this. He actually wanted to do it. He could conceivably go from there into something truly interesting, like mortuary work or maybe working with the esteemed

Coroner's Department in San Francisco. The Coroner's Department is the only one in the nation that requires the guys running the meat wagon around to wear a uniform. John was all into that kind of fascism, but he usually looked too weird to conform. He had suddenly found his chance to conform, and he had taken it. If he wanted to live his life trying to balance the scales with that, it was his problem.

One of the amazing things about the shell of a bookish observational nerd is that it allows you to rationalize some pretty nasty stuff. I can maintain plausible deniability with this mask. I thought John should be allowed to keep up the tank and take care of it, because I think he loved it. The dedication that consumed him when he got that job impressed me, and he was a better person for it.

I never walked in to the Cadaver Tank. I didn't particularly feel like breathing formaldehyde that day, so I told John to forget it. I can honestly look you in the face and say, "I don't know that such a thing exists because I never saw it."

9

Information Gladly Given But Safety Requires Avoiding Unnecessary Conversation

T he turning of the key happened in an extremely small way, as most key-turnings do. This one was a tad smaller than others, as it involved a door opened by our roommate Samantha.

Samantha was especially interesting in the morning in various states of makeup smearage. It was an amazing task to figure out what effect she'd been going for the previous night after it had been splattered roughly with water and rubbed with a towel. She usually stumbled upon Lloyd, John and me talking in the kitchen while fixing breakfast. She didn't seem to sleep much, but then again we never saw her most of the day.

"What're you guys doing tonight?" asked Sam, lurching blearily into the kitchen. Sam was wearing a black silk kimono embroidered with green and red dragons. She headed straight for the coffee pot.

"Nothing on my end," I said.

"I'm free," said John.

"I dunno, what's up?" asked Lloyd. "There's a Black Mass tonight, and if I skip it for some thrilling gothic event,I could miss out on having sex."

"There's some band coming into town," said Sam, shooting Lloyd a look. "Jimmy needs the club to have a lot of people, seems they used to be big news somewhere and Jimmy knew them from way back. Jimmy's just pissed so many people off..."

"You need to pack the place for whatever reason." I said.

"Yeah," said Sam. She looked kind of like a raccoon with a black lion's mane, dressed in a Ministry t-shirt and panties.

"Are we on the list?" I asked.

"Of course you are!" she said.

We all looked at each other, and looked back at Sam.

"OK, I'll get you drink tickets."

The bar Sam worked at had a strange little system of keeping track of employee drinks. They would issue so many tickets per night to the promoters, and these would be given out to the people who worked the events. Sam usually got five drink tickets. I think she'd figured out a way to whip up a black market in them.

"I'll give you five tickets each," she said.

We all looked at her in surprise.

"OK," said Lloyd. He heartily approved of subversion of systems to his own advantage.

"I'm there," said John. He was always scamming something, why should this be any different?

"Cathy drinks virgin drinks, I can get those free," I said. "I'll go, even though Cathy doesn't like going out."

"Will she take convincing?" asked Sam.

"Probably not," I lied.

###

We opted out of catching the Haight Street bus and decided to grab a 38 Geary bus instead. Lloyd heard that something weird had happened to a friend of his on the 38 line, but he wouldn't elaborate.

"Some things are better left unsaid," said Lloyd.

"This corset is too fucking tight," said Cathy.

"When does the bus get here?" asked John.

"We're late, and the next Fulton bus might be the last bus," I said."It's scheduled to be here in a minute, but MUNI never runs on time. At any rate, the 38 runs all night."

No sooner had the words come out of my mouth than a lumbering white and orange behemoth of a city bus came hurtling over the top of the hill from the direction of the sea. It didn't even stop for a yellow light a block away, and it zipped through the intersection towards us.The driver expertly applied the brakes and scooted the bus neatly into the special bus stop lane at the corner that was like every other block on the route.

The door flipped open and a thin Chinese man in his mid-forties looked down upon us. He was wearing a brown MUNI uniform and baseball cap. This alone made him seem nerdlike, but his large horn-rimmed glasses enhanced the bookish effect. His coarse black hair jutted out like evil straw from his cap, and his clean-shaven face made his eyes seem to transmit the urgency he was projecting.

"Hurry up," he hissed. "We got a schedule to keep!"

We all bundled on board and started to pay.

"Move all the way to back," he spat at us. "You ride free, I just have to get to garage on time!"

Confused, we moved towards the back of the bus, and then moved more quickly because the frantic driver had whipped the bus out into the street again and had brought the bus up to full speed within about six seconds. I grabbed onto a pole to steady myself and found myself violently spun around by the force of the bus's takeoff. As I clung to the pole, I looked back at the driver's face staring nervously in the mirror at us and just below a large sign that had been posted:

"Information gladly given but safety requires avoiding unnecessary conversation."

Safety? The man was mad, you could see it in his eyes. At least he was obsessed about keeping the bus on schedule. This was a clear deviation from MUNI policy, which stated that MUNI was only allowed to arrive thirty minutes after you need it to be there.We adjusted for the speed and proceeded towards the back of the cavernous bulk of the bus.

The bus was a two-car bus, and almost immediately at the second car the atmosphere changed noticeably.The first thing I noticed was that some taggers had really gone over the back of the bus. Taggers were a small force of kids who patrolled the buses with one-inch-wide felt tip pens, swirling initials, gang signs, or some other unspeakable sigil. That's exactly what the entire last twenty feet of bus looked like, like someone had covered it in unholy hieroglyphs. Every square inch was scrawled upon, and only the very last seats remained untouched.We gingerly made our way back to the rear of the car.

"All the way to the back!" screamed the driver. The bus lurched ahead and shot through an intersection.

I looked at my watch, hoping that maybe we'd get to the club before midnight — but one glance at my watch dashed all hopes of that. It was almost exactly tomorrow.

Cathy looked around at the bus and the swirling sigils painted across the entire back half of the bus, and she was the first to notice.

"These aren't gang symbols," she said. "This is all graffiti in Chinese."

"I think you're right," said Lloyd. "This gives me the creeps. Chinese people don't do graffiti."

"Thanks for clarifying that stereotype for us, Lloyd," I said wryly.

"No, I'm serious," said Lloyd. "The only reason to cover anything with writing for Chinese people is some kind of…"

A thump and a shriek interrupted Lloyd. It had just turned exactly midnight. We jerked our heads to the front of the car, as Lloyd finished his sentence.

"…supernatural reason."

As we looked ahead in the first car, it seemed as if fog swirled around in the middle of the first car. A ghostly figure formed in the fog. The only definite things about it were the eyes, small glowing pinpricks in the fabric of reality.The figure began to take on a vaguely humanoid shape, and seemed to notice us. It started moving back through the bus towards us as the scent of death permeated the bus.

It didn't walk towards us. It hopped. For some reason, this was laughable and terrifying all at the same time.

From the little I know about Chinese ghosts and vampires, it is almost universal that they hop towards their victims. The Chinese did not ignore the condition of rigor mortis when recalling their folklore, and it is rigor mortis that makes the corpses of their legends unable to move in anything other than short hops. Unfortunately, we weren't being faced with a corpse at the moment. Cathy let out a slight gasp and then fainted. She was, after all, wearing a corset and had probably just hyperventilated – she had chronic asthma. I know that my own breath was coming rather rapidly.

"Shit!" screamed the manic little Chinese driver as he stomped on the gas. He fiddled with the front sign while he drove, until a sign swung around that said "Sorry, No Passengers."

The hopping ghost got to the middle of the bus. The bus careened about wildly, so that the ghost was continually off balance.The instant the ghost tried to cross the threshold to the second section of the bus, blue sparks shot out from the walls and the ceiling of the bus, and the twisted wraith was thrown back into the front part of the bus.

The hopping ghost had half of his head shaved, in a line that connected both of his ears across the front of his head. The back part of his head ended in a long braid of hair that hung down to the middle of his back. This hair was moldy yellow, as if it had turned white and then gotten stained with water. The smooth face revealed skin peeling away from the bones of the face, a nose half eaten away and lidless eyes that could not keep in the evil reddish pinpricks that the ghost used to see. The corpse wore moldy white cotton pants and a tunic that had loops of cloth holding it closed. Some of the cloth strips were rotten, and you could see the corpse's rib cage underneath.

"Holy shit, it's a Chinese ghost," said Lloyd.

"Fuck this, man. We're close to the club. Let's get off," said John.

We looked at the ghost. It had ceased trying to get to us and had now turned its attention to the manic little man driving our bus. The ghost hopped forward one hop towards the man, as the man looked backwards at the corpse advancing on him. He didn't seem that scared, now that I think about it.

He stomped on the gas pedal of the bus. The bus lurched forward. The corpse stumbled backwards and was trapped against a wall of blue sparks. An unholy shriek went up, and the corpse jumped forward yet again.

The driver, fully in control of himself, sped up again and repeated the procedure.

Hop. Stomp. Lurch. Stumble. Shriek. This pattern happened at least four times.

"I think this guy knows what he is doing," I said.

"What do you mean?" said John.

Hop. Stomp. Lurch. Stumble. Shriek.

"Well, he seems to know how to keep the ghost from getting him," I said.

At this moment, the bus slowed to a stop. We looked up at the front, where the driver set the parking brake in a hiss of pressurized air, and he flung open the door. The ghost hopped once forward, then started lurching forward again. The little bus driver went down into a crouch. He had a handful of MUNI transfers in his hand, and he appeared to be writing frantically on them. His hand flew as the ghost lurched closer and closer to him.

"Shit! That thing's going to get the driver!" said John.

"I think he's writing out a sutra," said Lloyd.

"A what?" said John.

"It's a Buddhist thing," said Lloyd.

The corpse was four feet away from the driver.

"Fuck this!" said John. "There's a back door, and I'm using it!"

John moved towards the back door, as the little man started to spring into action. Moving with lightning speed, he dodged the clumsy swinging of the ghostly corpse and used his free hand to rip away the topmost transfer. He brought it to his lips and licked the back of it, then thrust his arm out in some kind of martial arts move to smack the transfer directly onto the forehead of the corpse. It stuck there, covering the eyes of the corpse.

The corpse froze in its tracks.

"Oh man," said Lloyd.

The little bus driver appeared to relax, and then he smacked another transfer into the corpse's chest. The stench of decay wafted past our nostrils. Cathy stirred a little bit from her faint, and opened her eyes just after the viscous fog that the corpse had turned into dissipated.

"What happened?" she asked.

"You fell asleep," I said.

"I had the weirdest dream," she said.

"I have to talk to the bus driver, my love," I said. "Get off the bus and I'll meet you on the curb."

Cathy got up behind me and moved off the bus as I walked forward to the bus driver.

"What the hell was that?" I asked the driver as he turned back towards his seat.

"What did it look like?" he shot back. "It was a ghost, a hopping vampire."

"Those don't exist," I said.

He laughed.

"Keep on believing that, white boy," he said. "Why do you think MUNI is always late?"

"Oh, come on," I said. "You're trying to tell me that hopping vampires appear on every MUNI bus at midnight and make the entire system run slowly?"

The man merely turned around and pointed at the sign behind him.

"Information gladly given but safety requires avoiding unnecessary conversation."

10

The Nightclub

Sam was pissed that we hadn't made it the previous week, but she put us on the guest list for next week anyway. We arrived at the nightclub just in time for the doors to open, meaning we were the first people there. Nine o'clock is such an awkward time to arrive anywhere in the nightclub scene.

Samantha sat at the door when we walked up. She looked us up and down, and consulted a list in front of her. "Well, I recognize you folks, and imagine that! Your name is on the list. Lloyd, John, Cathy, and Derwood darling…" said Sam, in an exaggerated, campy mother-in-law voice.

"Very funny, Sam," I said.

The nightclub ritual had begun.

We walked down the narrow stairway of the Café Du Sutro, a swank new club that occupied an old speakeasy on Market Street. Lloyd had huffed around a large statue and looked at me ominously when we'd gotten off the bus. He clutched a flyer he had torn from the statue and showed it to me as we walked down the stairs to below the level of Market Street.

"'The Trenchcoat Mafia'? What kind of a name for a goth band is that?" said Lloyd.

"Who knows?" I said.

The entrance at the bottom of the ornate stairwell was nice. There was enough room for three people to walk comfortably abreast, and burnished redwood handrails helped you down the stairs until they ended at a slight curve and melded into the wall at the bottom. The wood paneling was thick and darkly stained, with about a hundred years' worth of shellac layered over it. A glass case displayed a poster for the featured band or event — many different events were held here, and there was even a full kitchen that could prepare dinner for a hundred or so. I'd been here before for a dinner party on the anniversary of the sinking of the Titanic, featuring the fateful dinner menu of that evening and a band playing the doomed playlist from all those years ago.

The inside was a good place for that type of event. Ornately carved wood gleamed from every corner of the large seating area, and in the back room a stage dominated the ballroom. A massive mahogany bar sprawled about the seating area. I loved the place for the scent of polished wood and smoky scotch. Well, for at least the first hour of it. In a few hours it would be packed with drunken twentysomethings and things would smell considerably different. For now, we seemed to be standing in the way.

In the dance area, the DJ cued up something decidedly un-goth. He was playing '1999' by Prince. Lloyd and John started twitching. Cathy looked at me.

"There's nobody here yet," I said."Maybe no one will know we heard this song."

At the moment I said that, I got a prickling at the back of my neck and turned around. A shadowy figure sat in a booth near the back.Though he was nobody I recognized, the feeling I had was familiar.

"Hey, kids!" shouted Jimmy the Speed Freak. Jimmy wore PVC pants that nobody had ever seen him out of. He smelled awful and his shaved head only made him look more skeletal. Jimmy ran the club night, so we had to be nice. "So you're sitting here grooving to Prince?"

"No," I said. "You are. I was just about to complain what a shitty nightclub this was to the owner."

"Hey, feel the love!" said Jimmy. "Here, have a drink ticket."

\#\#\#

Over the course of the night, we watched the entire bar walk by our table. We were tucked far back in the darkest depths of the club space, and everyone eventually came back out of curiosity or some other impulse. The first pair to walk by were some slightly overweight girls kissing each other. They wore black spandex tights and leather vests, with East German police hats on.

"Some people shouldn't wear spandex," said Lloyd. "Although I approve of women kissing each other."

The next up was a girl dressed in a black business suit with a mustache painted on. She walked around talking to nobody, and though she presented a striking figure she seemed to look down her nose at everyone that approached her.

"That's Julie Newmar," said John. "No, not Catwoman, but that's her name. She designs clothes. She's got a broomstick rammed up her ass -she thinks she's God's gift."

"What do her clothes look like?" I asked.

"Never seen any of them," replied John.

The next person making the rounds was the DJ. He told us he was taking a pee break, but we all knew he was going to powder his nose. He stopped by on his way to the bathroom, as if we absolutely needed to know he had to piss.

"Hey, folks, how's it goin'! I'm glad you could stop by, Sam told us the weird thing you said happened last week that kept you — bus trouble, right?"

"Yes," I replied. "You could say that."

"Yeah, alright, I have to pee, you know? But I'll be back by. We'll talk more!"

"Yeah, see you," said Lloyd.

"What's his deal?" I asked Lloyd.

"I dunno," said Lloyd. "I know he's the biggest buyer of ice for personal use in San Francisco, though."

"Yuck," I said.

"Hey, tweakers are people too," said Lloyd.

The DJ came bouncing out of the bathroom, totally oblivious to our presence, and hugged a transvestite close to the door. The tranny suddenly appeared alarmed by this turn of events but smiled nonetheless in the sliding grimace that is a combination of severe stress and application of petroleum jelly to the surfaces of the teeth. I felt sorry for the hapless person as the sweaty DJ bounced off towards the DJ booth.

Another couple walked by. This time, we were graced by the presence of Lord and Lady Darkling. The first time I had been introduced to them, it was all I could do to keep from laughing. They usually wore completely black Victorian mourning clothes from the late 1800's. This being San Francisco, such things were available because some people had attics that still held old clothes from after 1906. I recalled being able to buy some of these gowns of rotten lace out of garage sales, and I felt sad that a couple of twits like this pair had been able to buy them and take them out to clubs where they'd be torn and destroyed eventually. We nodded to them.

"What a pair of obnoxious assholes," spat John. "I hate people who have money and flaunt it. They buy every single one of their friends."

"What?" I asked."I don't think they have much money left, after buying those antique mourning clothes."

"They're trust fund kiddies," sneered John.

"OK," I shrugged.

The next person to walk by was Ontario. Ontario was a girl who hated to be called by her real name, and decided to name herself after a Canadian province because she thought it was a pretty word. Unfortunately, it led to a lot of jokes about her rather portly collection of PVC wear.

"Don't they make a lot of sausage in Ontario?" asked Lloyd.

"No, that's just what happens when you put an entire province inside a PVC dress."

"Not every guy wants to live in Ontario, it's way too large to appreciate all of it."

"I wonder if it's hot and steamy in Ontario, or if it's cold and rocky?"

We all laughed and John snorted Coke and whiskey through his nose.

"OUCH!"

###

The entire time we sat there talking and watching the hapless drug-addled nightlife file by, a lurking shadow grew in the corner. I spotted him a couple of times, a brooding figure who sat alone in a booth close to the door to the men's bathroom. Spotting him from across the room, I kept an uneasy eye on him from the beginning, through the flashing lights and swirling cheap PVC-eating chemical fog the club used. I only failed to watch him once, and that proved to be the most crucial time of all in recalling the scene later for the authorities.

I had become convinced that the man in the booth was not a threat or problem slightly before midnight. I took my eyes off of him about 11:45PM. The deejay played an older song by The Smiths, and Lloyd decided that this was a good time for him to take a leak. He got to his feet with the weight of tequila, and shambled off towards the door net to the growing pool of darkness. The DJ then decided he would play an extra-long version of "Sex Dwarf", by Soft Cell.

Almost as soon as the song started thumping through the speakers, the gunfire began.

I looked across the room. I saw Jimmy backing away from the booth in the corner, and then the sudden flash of more gunfire in the strobe lights of the club. Jimmy flew backwards from the booth, and the dark figure stood up and started shooting people with a pair of dark black pistols he had. People dodged him as he walked over to the deejay booth, and the stunned deejay backed against the wall, screaming. The dark figure shot him through the forehead as he squealed out his dying words — hopefully they were something like, "I didn't mean to play Prince, I'm sorry."

The black-clad figure turned as a few rivetheads tried to sneak up on him. He blasted at them with both pistols, taking at least one out of the game forever. I saw brain matter fly across a spotlight. He turned to face Lady Darkling and she swooned into the arms of Lord Darkling. Lord Darkling got this strange look on his face as he wrestled with a decision and then dropped his girlfriend and ran for the door. A casual shot to the back of the head sent his face smashing into the wall in a thousand bloody pieces.

The figure turned and advanced on me.

Along the way, he came upon Julie Newmar, who had tripped across a fallen rivethead in a bid to get free. As the shot that killed Julie Newmar echoed through the club and Marc Almond wailed about luring disco dollies to a life of vice, I turned to face my tablemates. It was all happening so quickly that we were still sitting there stunned.

"Under the table!" I yelled at John, who was sitting slack-jawed.

"Now!" I screamed at Cathy. She quickly slid under the table, and I slid under, too, with her between me and the booth. I shielded her best as I could. I had to grab John by the pants and haul him under.

The man walked closer to our table, and I saw a pair of large legs in fishnet stand in front of our booth. The music faded off now, and the sound of sirens echoed from outside, from somewhere down the street.

"I know you're killing everyone," the owner of the legs said, "but please consider sparing me and taking me with you when you leave. I give really good head."

A shot rang out, and the owner of the legs toppled backwards to stare directly at me. I couldn't recognize Ontario from the face that had been shot off, but rather by the fact that she was still wearing that awful sausage-casing dress.

The legs of the gunman came up to the booth and I heard Cathy sobbing hysterically next to me. I realized that we were probably going to die in the next few minutes unless a miracle happened, and I held Cathy tighter. I heard the sound of a weapon being reloaded and cocked above the table covering us.

A shot rang out.

The man sat solidly onto Ontario's chin, forcing the top of her empty head into a puddle of gore and splashing brains and blood in my face. He wheezed once and fell over backwards as another pair of black-clad legs strode towards our table and tossed a smoking Glock pistol onto the chest of the twitching maniac.

"The things that happen when I have to go pee," said Lloyd. "There's a piece of brain in my cocktail."

Behind Lloyd, through a broken window, I thought I saw the statue outside turn and look in at us.

11

Don't Call it Frisco

Cathy was never the same after watching the massacre in the bar. None of us were, really. But she took it the worst. Until now, we hadn't been presented with death, real and unadulterated. It's one thing to suspect your landlord is a serial killer, but this? I thought about that nervously while the police drove us to the station. They had to book Lloyd on a murder charge, and he was released on his own recognizance. On his entrance processing to the jail facility, Lloyd wrote down 'Satanist' as his religion and 'Drug dealer' as his occupation. The person processing the papers looked Lloyd straight in the eye as he held the door open for him. We gave Sam's post office box as an address so that nobody would find the house, to which we made our slow, painful way home.

That didn't stop the reporters from finding us. Immediately, the telephone number was compromised, and the telephone company was slow to turn on Caller ID for us. We took to screening our calls over an answering machine. I inadvertently picked up the phone one evening and found myself explaining to CNN that the gunman wasn't 'Goth', he was a neo-fascist white-power rivethead I'd seen chasing after some girl there. We received a death threat. I kept that from Cathy.

We'd had an examination, by doctors, when we came out of the scarred remnants of the nightclub. Looking back on it, she did the sanest thing of all. The rest of us kept the secrets as if they would save us. Cathy decided she needed therapy. There wasn't a doubt, actually. When the police officer took her statement, she looked up at the woman with a thousand-yard stare and said simply, "I am going to need lots and lots of therapy."

This turned out to be to our advantage. This got out to the news media, mostly because Cathy couldn't say anything else for about three days.We blundered out of the courthouse to be blinded by flashbulbs and had microphones stuck into our faces. Cathy looked dead at the camera and said it.

"I am not sure how much therapy I'm going to need to get over this."

###

The first calls were from the media, but others managed to get the number too. When we first got back the day after the shootings, we were in the house for about fifteen minutes when the phone rang and we let the answering machine pick it up. It was a doctor calling from Beverly Hills. He wanted something to boost his practice, and give him a little bit of publicity. This upset me a little bit, until I found out we would be flown to Los Angeles to stay at his ranch for a private session. Lloyd listened to the message and took down the number on the chalkboard in the kitchen, while I set about making coffee. John sat at the table rolling a joint, as he decided he just needed something to calm his nerves a bit.

"Fuck yeah," said Lloyd. "A free plane ride and a stay at some doctor's ranch in L.A.? I'd be there in a second."

"She's not doing too well, Lloyd," I said. "She really needs to talk to someone about this."

"I'm not saying she doesn't," said Lloyd, "but why can't I get the shrink with the cushy ranch in L.A.? I shot someone, you know. I might never recover my innocence."

John and I both kind of stopped and stared at Lloyd for a second.

"OK, so you guys can see through my bullshit. What I need is a lawyer. I'm going to go talk to my dealer friend, he has a good one."

Lloyd walked out, and I walked upstairs to tell Cathy about our windfall.

###

Cathy was not well.

When I walked upstairs to tell her about the doctor, I found her sobbing in our bed. We had made our room as comfortable as possible when we moved in, buying a large iron sleigh bed and a feather mattress for it. She was curled up into a fetal position on the bed, sobbing uncontrollably. I might have done the same, if I hadn't been happy that another crappy DJ was dead.

"Cathy?" I asked.

More sobbing.

"Honey, it's going to be okay," I said, as I settled down into the bed next to her.

"N-n-no," she sobbed. "It's n-n-not okay."

"We're fine, Cathy," I said. "It could have been worse, but Lloyd saved us."

Cathy looked at me through red eyes. She had stripped off her gore-spattered dress and tossed it into the trash can. I stroked her back as she convulsed, crying.

"Lloyd only shot him so he wouldn't g-g-get shot," Cathy sobbed. "Lloyd only c-c-cares about himself."

I had to admit that she had a point.

"You have a point," I said. "So why look a gift horse in the mouth?"

"W-w-we should be dead!" she said. "Why aren't we dead?"

"I don't know, hon," I said. "I really don't know."

"I f-f-feel awful," she said. "I feel like the world has g-g-gone mad."

"Well, maybe we can get you some help, my love," I said as I stroked her raven-black hair.

###

We flew into Los Angeles a day later. I was extremely worried that Cathy was suicidal, and I wanted to make sure she was still alive to take advantage of the doctor's kind offer. We rode in a small dart-like jet with two engines near the back of the fuselage. There were four seats to each row, and we had been booked into first class by the kindly shrink. I figured that if he practiced in Beverly Hills, he could probably afford it. I didn't complain, but rather I downed four colas mixed with Jack Daniels in the fifty-five minutes it took us to reach Los Angeles. I handed my glass back to the stewardess as we passed over a church's parking lot that had "HOME OF THE FAITH DOME" in large letters stenciled across the tarmac so you could see it from the flight path. Cathy sat quietly, barely acknowledging the steward who asked her to bring her seat back and tray table to the full upright and locked position.

We trudged through the marble and glass airport, passing through genuine potted palm trees to the contrast of the grim and humorless baggage claim area. I led Cathy to the carousel as our bags were spat out of the conveyor hole onto the rotating steel merry-go-round of Samsonite and American Tourister. A woman with a small dog stared at us, and as we were walking out to the pickup zone, I saw a man dressed in a sharp black uniform with a small cap standing there, looking around at the crowd holding a small sign with Cathy's name on it. We walked towards him.

"Hello," I said. "You must be our driver."

"Buzz off, kid," said the man.

"No, seriously, you're waiting for us." I said.

The man looked at us a second, and then a young Japanese girl walked up to us from literally out of nowhere.

"Do you mind if we take your picture with us?" she said.

"No," I said, slightly irritated.

"You just look so interesting, are you a rock star?" she asked.

I sighed.

"Come on," said the limo driver.

###

Limo drivers are very different from taxi drivers, I discovered. For one thing, limo drivers do not talk to you unless you ask them something. If you talk to them enough, they might loosen up and start talking to you a little bit more.

The general rule of thumb, however, is that they should not speak unless spoken to. I decided to chat the limo driver up.

 · "So, do you work for Dr. Lechter?" I asked. Our doctor was one Dr. Frederick Lechter, an eminent German-born psychologist who evidently had some notoriety in Hollywood circles. I'd done some research on him; he was supposedly extremely good at what he did.

"No sir," said the limo driver.

"What, is there a limo company you call up, just like a taxi company?" I asked. I had no idea how limousine services worked.

"Yes sir," said the limo driver.

"Can you stop calling me sir?" I asked.

"If you wish, sir," said the limo driver, and then he caught himself. "Sorry."

"No problem, I'm just not a very formal person."

"Me neither." said the limo driver. "I just have to keep to myself because I drive around a lot of famous people and they don't like chitchat."

"Ah, good," I said. "You're not a starched automaton."

"A what?" asked the driver.

"A robot," I said.

"Heh, oh yeah," he said. "You're pretty cool, where are ya from?"

"San Francisco," I said. "And yourself?"

"I'm from Boston," said the limo driver.

"Boston, I have an aunt there," I said.

"Yeah, I miss it," he said. "I bet it's nothing like Frisco though."

I cringed. He'd said the 'F' word.

"It's not nice to call it 'Frisco,'" I said.

"Oh yeah?" he said. "Sorry, I've always called it Frisco."

I grated my teeth.

"It's just a tradition," I said. "That's just not what it's called."

"What, there ain't a law against calling it Frisco, is there?" he asked.

I was beginning to get the feeling he was trying to piss me off.

"As a matter of fact, there is," I said. "A twenty-five dollar fine too, but most people don't recognize the authority of the person who proclaimed it."

"Who's that?" asked the limo driver.

"Norton the First," I replied."Emperor of the United States and Protector of Mexico."

"Is that a fact?" asked the driver, looking at me in his rear view mirror. He looked worried for my sanity. "I ain't never heard of him."

"He died in the 1800's," I said. "Not many people outside of San Francisco know who he is."

"Is that a fact?" the limo driver repeated. I could sense him moving towards his cell phone, ready to call 911.

"Yes," I said. "It's a fact."

We finished our journey in silence.

###

We came to a stop at the end of a long driveway after turning off of what seemed to be a major thoroughfare. I say that it seemed to be a major thoroughfare because the house we pulled up to seemed utterly isolated—I couldn't believe that this was on the outskirts of Hollywood in the hills. The chauffeur dutifully put his limo driver mask back on and carried our bags to the door, where Dr. Lechter greeted us.

"Ah, good, you're on time," he said. "I fixed dinner for us."

I don't like psychologists. I always feel like they are trying to analyze me. I once told this to a psychologist, and he just looked at me over the top of his glasses and said, "That's very interesting."

Dr. Lechter was nothing like that.

"Come in!" he said. "Make yourselves at home! Tell me a little bit about yourselves!"

Cathy looked around at the house and started shaking a little bit.

Dr. Lechter lived in what could be termed a "Spanish Ranch" house. It was built around a central courtyard, the way I've heard houses in Spain are built. From the outside, the adobe walls and Spanish tiled roof made the place look much smaller than it actually was. When we walked into the front door, the living room and foyer were bigger that the entire first floor of the house we now occupied in San Francisco.

We sat down at a dinner table, and then Dr. Lechter asked us if we liked tofu. This made Cathy shake a little bit more, as she is allergic to soybeans.

"So, tell me how things are in Frisco!" said Dr. Lechter.

I gritted my teeth and told him.

###

In the end, Dr. Lechter and I had a private conference while Cathy lay resting in the guest bedroom.

"How do you think she's holding up?" he asked.

"Not very well," I said. "She's dwelling a little bit more than usual on death."

Dr. Lechter snorted. "Does she always dwell on death?"

"Well, she's morbid like me," I replied. "I know she's seen dead people before, but I don't think she's had gore from exploding bodies cover her before."

"Right," said Dr. Lechter, and he just looked at me.

"I mean, now she's just repeating that we should be dead," I said.

"So tell me what happened," said Dr. Lechter.

I related the whole sordid tale, starting with the door to the club, the bad DJ, through the vapid people, and ended it with Lloyd blowing the guy's head off with a Glock.

"Your friend, Lloyd, how is he holding up?" asked Dr. Lechter.

"Lloyd's fine," I replied.

"He shot a man in the head, I'd imagine that would mess with his mind a bit," said Dr. Lechter.

"You'd have to know Lloyd," I said. It was the truth.

"Well, if he needs any help, tell him to call me," Dr. Lechter said. He seemed genuinely concerned.

"I dunno," I said. "If you talked to Lloyd, you might end up needing a shrink yourself."

Dr. Lechter laughed, and then he turned serious.

"I'd like to suggest that Cathy stay with me for a short while. Maybe a month," he said.

I cocked my head and looked at him.

"Why do you think that's needed?" I asked.

"Well, it may be good for her," he started. "Traumatic experiences can sometimes be lessened by a so-called 'vacation'. Consider it something like that."

I thought about it.

"I have to go back to work in a three days," I said. "I want to stay until then."

"Okay," said Dr. Lechter.

###

I called the house in San Francisco after my conversation with Dr. Lechter. The answering machine picked it up, and I spoke in an urgent tone attempting to leave a message, but Lloyd's burly voice cut the machine off and greeted me.

"Hey, man, what's up?"

"Cathy's going to be staying here a while," I said. "I'm coming home in three days."

"Really? Is she totally nutso?" asked Lloyd.

"No, she is not 'totally nutso', Lloyd. I think she'll be safer down here."

"Safe from what?" asked Lloyd.

"You know what I'm thinking, Lloyd?" I asked.

"No, tell me." he said.

"I think that all the insanity lately is because of your fucking statues," I said.

There was a pause and silence, then Lloyd spoke.

"You might be right," said Lloyd.

"I think that when I come back, we're going to figure out a way to stop all this bullshit," I said.

I could feel Lloyd's trepidation from five hundred miles away, oozing through the phone at me.

"You mean to break the sigil," he said, flatly.

"I think that will fix a lot of things," I said. "And I don't think we have much time before all Hell breaks loose."

Lloyd snorted.

"And you think I want to go along with this?" he said.

"You're going to die too, if this is what you claim it is," I said.

"You have a point."

"So, are we agreed?" I asked.

"Yes," said Lloyd.

"I'll see you in a week, then," I said.

"I'll see you then. Be careful, man."

I hung up the phone. I felt certain that everything that had happened to me—the statues, the man jumping off the Golden Gate, having a serial killer for a landlord, the hopping ghost on the bus, the nightclub shootout, and Cathy's insanity—was intertwined somehow, a latticework of cause and effect that all depended on exactly one thing. It all revolved around the sigil that some mystic asshole had carved into the City, after the great earthquake had cleaned the slate for him. It was time for things to change, and I was at the point where I didn't want anything but a semblance of normalcy (whatever that was) in my life again.

I found myself sketching pentagrams in the margins of the yellow pages as I looked up occult shops in the Hollywood phone directory at midnight. I copied down several addresses, and then padded off to bed with visions of leering statues dancing in my head.

It was time to put an end to all of this, but at the time I had no idea how long it would take.

12

Killer Bees

I set out the next day under the pretense of shopping on Melrose. The doctor dropped me off in from of a strange shop that held a trepanning tool that I fell in love with almost instantly. The place sold medical antiques, and the doctor had suggested it after a long talk at breakfast had revealed an interest in old dental stands from the twenties.

The shop held my attention effectively while the doctor drove away, and then I walked out towards the bright sunlight and Hollywood Boulevard.

San Francisco and Los Angeles have two distinctly separate energies. A long walk is nothing at all to someone from San Francisco, but in Los Angeles it just isn't done. I quickly found out why this was the case, being in Los Angeles for the first time in my life. It's really fucking hot in Los Angeles and Hollywood.

I had lived in the south before moving to San Francisco, but southern heat was more likely to make you curl up into a pile of sweat. As I walked up towards the hills of Hollywood, I saw a shimmering heat haze that I'd previously only seen in the fields of Georgia in the humid air. The dryness made it vibrate with an urgency it had never had in the state I grew up in. It was like having the moisture leached out of me by a giant fruit dehydrator. I cursed softly and trudged north. I thought about stopping for some zinc sunblock.

I had gone about seven blocks when something ahead caught my attention.

A man ran out of a building up ahead in the shimmering heat, and started tearing up the pavement towards me. He was moving at a pretty fast clip. I watched him cover a block and a half between us, and then he started to slow his pace. He slowed and turned to look behind him.

"What's up?" I asked. He looked frightened.

"Bees..." he gasped.

"Bees?" I said.

"Yeah, a whole swarm of them," he said. "They were in my back yard and chased after me."

"They chased you?" I asked.

"Yeah, well, they were all over this tree and I was looking at it and suddenly they all started flying at me," he gabbled. It was increasingly obvious that he was terrified.

I looked ahead. If he were correct and wasn't on any drugs, there was a swarm of bees waiting between me and the shop I had picked out to visit. As a matter of fact, the shop should have been about four blocks ahead, and the bees were about two blocks.

"Are you on anything?" I asked the man.

"What?" he said. "What kind of a question is that?"

"Well, I know some stuff that will make you see bees," I said.

He laughed, which made me feel better. "I guess you're right, I never thought of it that way."

I looked at him. He seemed about my age, with the remnants of a clean-shaven face. His brown hair hung to his shoulders, and he looked at me through a pair of slightly bewildered brown eyes. He smiled a lot, and the only thing that distracted me about him was a tooth in his mouth that grew in at an odd angle. He was wearing black tank top stained with something dark red and some military black drawstring pants. I got the feeling he hadn't intended to be outside in the midst of people and meeting strangers.

"Let's walk back, they don't seem to be following you," I said.

"You're joking, right?" he said. "Those were killer bees. I'm calling animal control."

I suddenly realized that he was better equipped to deal with the situation than I was.

###

I realized that he was absolutely correct. It was creepy, having heard all my life about killer bees and now being faced with a whole angry swarm of them less than a block away from me. Killer bees weren't exactly killers, but they weren't nice either. Like every other morbid child, I had followed the advance of the Africanized honeybees up through South and Central America where they had begun as a research experiment that went awry in the nineteen seventies. Lurid stories I'd read in Newsweek and Reader's Digest as a child had fixed the images into my head of people being attacked by massive swarms merely for breathing wrong.

This was, in reality, a bit of an exaggeration. I read everything I possibly could about Africanized honeybees, and I knew that when they were crushed a pheromone was released that caused the remaining bees to attack the source of the odor. Bees mostly work by odors; having to find flowers to survive means that this only makes sense. If you were sensitive enough to smell a flower a mile a way, then how would you react to smelling your brother's guts smeared all over some huge moving thing thrashing at you? I understood this when I was younger, but then it was explained to me that it was more complicated than that — bees didn't smell flowers. I thought people were missing the point but now I thought about how I might just make it without crushing a bee, and I should be all right to get by. I still waited for the animal control people to get there, and then the pronouncement that came down made me even more nervous.

"They're gone," said the animal control officer.

"What?" asked the guy in the tank top. "Did you check everything?"

The man shucked his heavy leather gloves.

"Yeah, this is what they do. They're smart little buggers."

"You're joking, right?" said the concerned apartment dweller.

"Look, you probably stepped on one, that's why they seemed to chase you," he said. "When you closed the door leaving the building, they couldn't follow you so they backtracked and decided to find another place to swarm. We'll put the word out in the neighborhood, but I think they won't be back."

"I hope not, man, that was pretty freaky," said the man.

The animal control officer laughed.

"Yeah, these things are pretty freaky. We've been dealing with a lot of swarms lately, some people think they're them killer bees," he said. "It's just not true. All bees act like this, we've just been having a lot of swarms lately."

"Really?" I asked. "Why would that be?"

"I dunno, maybe sunspots?" said the man, grinning.

"I have to get going," I said. "I have somewhere to be."

###

I continued north on the street another few blocks. The street was exactly like a few million other streets in Los Angeles I came to see later: four lanes with a center divider lane. There were a lot of wide, flat, hot islands of concrete like this one. I noticed at this point that I was starting to move steadily uphill.

I moved past a bar on one corner, men darting in and out from behind a black curtain. I had the feeling that it wouldn't be too cool to duck in there. The bar itself seemed to have physical anger directed at the street and the world in general. I moved past a couple of restaurants and then I spied the sign of the shop I'd been looking for. I checked the address (1641 North Cahuenga, that was it) and moved towards the door.

On my way to the door, I became aware of several things. Between the shop and the restaurants I had just walked past was an entrance to a parking lot. I was aware of a space on my left and as I put my hand on the handle of the door I noticed that I had stepped on something. I tore my attention away from the statues in the window and the darkened interior of the shop to pick my foot up and look at the bottom of it. I noticed the humming almost immediately when I saw the crushed honeybee on the pavement.

"Aw, fuck," I thought, as I looked over into the parking lot. It took me half an instant to pinpoint the buzzing sound — the swarm producing it was about twenty feet away. Covering the tire of a brand new purple Volkswagen Beetle was a crawling, buzzing, writhing mass of insectile bodies, menacing little black and yellow darts that started to lift away from the tire and come towards me. I did the only sensible thing. I quickly opened the door and ran inside the shop.

A young woman with black hair streaked with red looked up. There were four other people in the shop and I walked briskly over to the counter. Blue eyes looked back at me with a rather bored expression past a nose ring, and her gum popped a couple of times. She had been reading, but wasn't now. The place reeked of incense, and scented smoke drifted everywhere.

"May I help you?" she asked brightly. I suddenly realized that I was expecting her to act like Denise, at the candle shop I visited with Lloyd on Divisadero in San Francisco. Denise was a flaming bitch to me, and she didn't even know who I was. I was somewhat taken aback, but I managed a frightened glance at the door. The sky seemed to grow cloudy outside, and I saw something splat against the smoky glass of the front door.

"Um," I said.

"Yeah?" she said.

"Bees," I said.

"I'll call animal control," she said, without missing a beat.

"The bees might find a way in," I said. "I stepped on one."

"Aw, shit," she said. "Did you have to?"

"I didn't notice until after I did it, sorry," I said.

"They attack when they smell dead bee," she said.

"I know," I said. "Coincidentally, I had a conversation about this very thing earlier today."

She tossed her hair back and I caught a scent of cloves or some kind of oil. She reached for the phone and pulled out the phone book as the buzzing outside got louder.

"Holy shit," she said, looking up with the phone cradled on her shoulder.

The bees were dive-bombing the door and the sidewalk outside. They were splatting against the door with a lot of force, and some of them were leaving wet smears across the smoked glass. This drove the rest of the bees into a frenzy, and the light kept diminishing as the insects covered the glass front of the store.

I turned to her.

"Keep dialing," I said.

Someone else in the store looked up. The store was a tiny room dominated by five or six display cases. Everything was painted black, and in some places I could see cloth covering wood-grain paneling. There were four people in the store, including the girl behind the counter. The other three suddenly looked very nervous.

"Wow, that's pretty weird," said a tall blond woman with sunglasses perched on her head.

"Yeah," chimed in a fat, furry, balding man wearing a pentacle.

"Uh oh," said the girl behind the counter, looking again at the door.

A bee was crawling in through the mail flap.

"Do joo hev a towel?" asked the last person in the store. This was a small brown woman with a thick accent and polyester pants. She looked to be about fifty or so, but she was very calm.

"Yes, I think I do," said the girl behind the counter as the bee leapt free of the mail slot with about six of its brethren. We all watched as more bees started to push open the mail slot.

"Hurry," hissed the woman and the girl behind the counter ran and started throwing things around in search of a towel. I grabbed the phone and started dialing, keeping an eye out for the bees. As I opened the directory, I turned to see the bees wobble around, searching for the scent of their dead comrade smeared across the bottom of my shoe.

One by one, they dropped to the floor as they hit the smoke-filled atmosphere of the pagan store. I remembered my readings about bees, and how smoke put them to sleep and made them less vicious. The bees dropped to the floor and buzzed around for a bit. We all backed away from them.

The counter girl came back with a wet towel and moved towards the door.

"Wow," said the counter girl, popping her gum. "I guess that opium incense did a number on them."

"Poppies," I croaked. "Poppies will make them sleep."

Only the counter girl laughed.

###

While we were waiting for the animal control, I asked the girl behind the counter a question.

"Do you know anything about sigils?"

"I know a bit," she said. "You want to make one?"

"I have to break one," I said.

She looked at me oddly.

"You don't strike me as the type that would be into that sort of thing. If you can't make them you probably can't break them," she said.

"Maybe I should tell you the whole story," I said.

"Yeah, maybe you should," she said.

It took about two more hours to explain everything to her, mostly because we kept getting interrupted by animal control explaining to us that everything was safe. I told her about Lloyd and she said that he seemed familiar to her, like she'd heard of him somewhere before. She'd never heard of John. I told her about the statues, and the incident on the bus, and then she suddenly freaked out when she found out I'd been in the infamous goth club shootout in San Francisco.

"Oh wow, your wife is the woman seeing Dr. Lechter?" she asked. She'd heard of Dr. Lechter. It seemed like everyone had.

"Yeah," I said. "And I want to try and get something done before she comes back to San Francisco, it's a little too weird there now."

"You think it's weird there?" she asked. "Look here. There's fucking bees attacking you everywhere you go here, man. Don't give me that shit. Things are weird all over. It's the end of the millennium."

"Well, I think there's something to this sigil thing, otherwise Lloyd wouldn't have brought it up," I said.

"You may be right about that, but I don't think I can help you," she said.

"What do you suggest?" I asked.

She looked at me a second as if I weren't thinking, and then made me

76

realize I wasn't thinking.

"If I were you, I'd go back to San Francisco and look up that wacky sorcerer bus driver you were telling me about. He sounds like someone who might be able to help you."

She was absolutely right.

13

Help and Disbelief

I sat at the kitchen table, slightly dazed. The past few weeks had not been kind to me, yet I knew that I must continue towards what we had to do. My flight from Los Angeles had been uneventful, but nonetheless I clutched my seat arms and searched outside the window for killer bees attacking the engines or Sasquatch trying to rip off the landing gear. The taxi ride home had seen me deposited unceremoniously in front of the huge old Victorian that served as our headquarters. I considered the heavy bars on the bottom apartment's window for a moment before hauling my bags up the stairs and into Sunday morning with Lloyd and John.

"How's Cathy?" asked Lloyd.

"She was better when I left," I said. "I guess that says something."

"Hey, funny," said Lloyd.

"What? I didn't get that. What would that say?" said John.

"Never mind," I said. "I was trying to be funny and it didn't work."

"Have some coffee, man," said Lloyd.

###

"So, how can we break the sigil?" I asked Lloyd.

"Well, these things are usually not done," he said.

"You're a Satanist, don't you know anyone who would know?" asked John.

"Yes, I do, as a matter of fact," said Lloyd. "I've already talked to him."

"What did he say?" I asked.

"He said that the only way to break it would be in a way that was proscribed by the person who cast the sigil. He said it wasn't a good idea in any event. All kinds of things could happen. Unfortunately, they are all less dangerous than what actually could happen if we didn't do this."

"What happens if we don't do this?" I asked.

"Well, the entire city will probably fall into a giant hole in the ground."

"Just the city?" I asked.

"I'm not sure, but he took off to New York yesterday afternoon after I told him about some of the stuff happening," said Lloyd.

"Great," I said. "No help."

"Well, how do we find out how to do this?" I asked. "Do we reverse-engineer the sigil? How can we do something like that?"

"Reverse what?" came a sleepy voice from the door. We all turned to look at Sam, in a nightshirt and holding a teddy bear.

###

"Let me get this straight just one more time," said Sam.

"OK," I said.

"There's a giant pentagram carved into the infrastructure of San Francisco by a group of rich weirdos who planned it all after the 1906 earthquake. It feeds off the deaths of anything in its immediate vicinity or inside of it, and at the turn of the millennium a giant hole is going to open up and swallow the entire city. That's right?"

"That's right," I said.

"And you three are trying to figure out a way to destroy this pentagram but you need to figure out how the people who cast this thing in the first place did it originally?"

"You got it," I said.

"And the nightclub thing was caused by it," she said.

"Yes," I said.

"That's got to be the stupidest thing I've ever heard," she said quietly. "Some of my friends died in that shithole."

"I wish I were lying, but it's true." I said. "We thought you might want to help us, but we're sorry if we offended you."

Sam stood there, with her teddy bear. She stared at me for a while.

"That's such an amazingly cheesy and stupid crock of shit that I know you couldn't have made it up," she said to me. "Lloyd has you by the nose, man."

"OK, then we won't tell you how the landlord is a serial killer," I said as she turned to go to her room.

"What?" Sam whipped around.

"The landlord is a serial killer," I said, matter-of-factly.

"Bull fucking shit!" said Sam.

"He's not lying, man," said Lloyd.

"Totally," said John.

Sam stood there and stared at us again.

"You are all three of you putting me on, and I can for once stand up to you three and prove you wrong," said Sam, as she walked out of the room.

I looked at Lloyd, then at John. We all looked towards the doorway, then we all jumped up and tried to make it through the door at once to try and stop Sam from knocking on the landlord's door.

Sam was already down the steps by the time we made it to the front door that she had locked. She was beating on the door as all three of us came up behind her, and the door swung open to reveal our landlord's cologne and finally our landlord, swathed in his usual attire.

"Oh, good, hello," he said. "I've been watching you. Do come in."

Sam walked in. John and I looked at Lloyd. He looked at us, and then walked in. John breathed a sigh of relief and then I was inside, feeling better that Lloyd felt safe going into the landlord's apartment. I felt that it must mean that Lloyd had his gun with him. My eyes adjusted to the light and I scanned the room looking for strange things.

A couch that was nearly black with dirt sat in a corner of the apartment. A couple of reclining lounge chairs, swathed in the plastic covering my grandmother used to have on her chairs, sat in front of the lower fireplace.

A small dining area that shared the space with the living room opened into a grimy kitchen. There was a door that was boarded up which obviously went to the upstairs, and then I realized that he could open it and walk up into where the door to the kitchen used to be and listen to us, maybe watch us. Not good, I thought.

Sam sat down on the couch and started talking to him.

"These guys say you're a serial killer," she said, matter-of-factly.

"You mean…" he started.

"Yes, you kill people."

"They didn't tell you?" he asked.

"Tell me what?" Sam asked.

"When you moved in?" he asked again. I suddenly realized he had given her time to slowly realize his game, and watch the expression of dawning terror on her face that he liked to see so much.

"You're a serial killer?" said Sam.

Our landlord smiled broadly, and nodded his head up and down vigorously. He loved this.

"Prove it," she said.

"The couch you are sitting on is covered in human fat," he said.

"Bullshit," said Sam.

"I have a lampshade I made here from human skin."

"So did Jimmy the club promoter, before he got shot in the spine."

"My sweater is soaked in human blood," he said.

"Hey, wait, I remember this," said Sam. "Weren't you guys trying to figure this out?"

"Yeah," I said, softly.

"OK, Mr. Serial Killer," said Sam. "Tell us or show us how you keep your sweater soaked in human blood without getting it on your other clothes or hands."

"OK," said the landlord cheerily. "I'm going to have to get my hands and face bloody to show you, but that's fine because I think today's treatment has gone rather splendidly."

"Treatment?" I asked.

"Yes, it's the only way I can control my psoriasis," he said.

"Human blood?" asked John. "How'd you know human blood would control it?"

"Wouldn't you like to know?" he said, and then he pulled off his bloody sweater to reveal an elaborate system of plastic tubing and a couple of hot water bottles.

"I made it myself," he smiled, sheepish.

"That's pretty obvious," I said.

"See, I have this tube here," he said, pointing to a tube going into one of the hot water bottles. "After I put the blood into something, I can siphon it off with this tube. It's a neat system."

"How do I know that's real human blood?" said Sam.

"What would be the point of it being fake?" said the landlord.

"These guys are bullshitting me, and they have you in on it," she said.

"Hang on," said the landlord, and he strode to the kitchen.

He returned with a human head.

"No way," said Sam.

"Yes, way," said the landlord, softly.

"Can I touch it?" she aked.

"By all means," said the landlord.

Sam poked at it.

"That's just a really good fake head, man." said Sam.

The landlord was starting to get pissed.

"Look here," said the landlord. "All of this stuff doesn't matter."

"What?" said Sam.

"What?" said John and myself. Lloyd had his hand halfway in his coat.

"Your friends are right," he said to Sam.

"About what?" she said. "About the fact you're all a bunch of assholes?"

"No," he said, barely able to control himself. "About the pentagram."

"What?" said all four of us at once.

"I know the names of the people who cast it. I know a lot. My family was once very big here in San Francisco."

"Fuck you guys," said Sam. "All this just to get me to believe in this stupid pentagram, this is really pushing it, you know?"

"Shut up, Sam," I said. "I want to hear what he has to say."

"My family was one of the first in San Francisco. As a matter of fact, my great-great-grandmother was one of the Donner Party," he said proudly. "She married and settled here, and our family has been here ever since. "

"Um hmmm," I said. Serial killers were notorious liars. How could we know he was telling the truth?

"At any rate, my great-great-grandfather was friends with some of the guys who built that pentagram," he said. "This was his house."

I took this opportunity to study our landlord. I hadn't really gotten a great look at him when I first met him, and the reason was obvious when you studied him closely. He looked like just about anyone you'd see on the streets. He was about five foot eleven, with blue eyes and sandy brown hair. He appeared to be in his late 30's, and had that weird inbred look most of the people I knew from Georgia had. There were plenty of imperfections in California, don't let the media image fool you. This man looked like someone from just about anywhere.

We moved out of his way as he gestured towards the kitchen.

"I have some of his things in there," he said. "He left a book here, too."

Lloyd and I looked at each other.

"A book?" said Lloyd.

"Yeah," said the landlord. "I've read it, but I can't understand it."

"Why not?" I said.

"Because it's in some kind of code," he said.

We left the landlord's apartment carrying a heavy handwritten diary, about eight and a half by eleven and bound in dark brown leather that was worn at the corners a very long time ago. As we trudged up the stairs I heard Sam muttering behind me.

"I still don't know what the fuck this is all about." she said quietly.

We reached the top of the stairs and I turned around. Sam came to a stop in front of me and I looked her straight in the eye.

"I don't care if you believe me or not," I said. "I give up. The only thing I know is that I've seen statues move, people die, Chinese vampires, killer bees and a big fucking loony blowing away a bunch of people I really didn't care for. I also think I've got enough to go on when I say that the end of this city is pretty much in sight if I don't do something soon, and I think I've got a chance to stop it if I can just find all the pieces. I have John and Lloyd, but you think we're just nuts.

"I don't know why I'm doing this. I think sometimes it's for Cathy, but she's out of harm's way now. The more I think about it, the more I think that I just don't want to see anything here sitting on the last plane of whatever dimension Hell exists on. I think I just like this city too much.

"Yeah, I think that too," chimed in Lloyd.

"Me three," said John.

"Jesus Christ," said Sam. "Am I just going insane because half my friends got killed, or are you making sense?"

The fog swept past the house and enveloped us as we all looked down at the book in Lloyd's hands.

14

It's a Cookbook

We sat in Lloyd's room bathed in the glow of a monitor as Lloyd posted something to his favorite Satanic website about breaking sigils. I was rather dubious of this. You see so many posts like that on websites. John sat on the bed, studying the heavy book.

"I can't make heads or tails of this," said John.

"I think that's the intent," said Lloyd. "But look at the format. That's not a diary, man."

"What?" said John.

"It's a cookbook," said Lloyd.

"A cookbook? Like this is some family cookbook?" said John.

"No, man. It's recipes, but it's not any recipes you'd want. I think that's someone's coded spells and rituals book."

"I think you're right," said John.

"What's that?" asked Sam, pointing at a piece of paper that floated out of the book.

John picked it up and turned it over.

"A dozen eggs, a pound of flour, a pound of butter..." he began.

"Ha ha, very funny," she said.

"No, really," he said. "Look."

John handed her the grocery list.

"Great." said Sam. "It's some turn of the century nutbag's recipes for grandma's roast leg of Grandpa and eyeball stew."

"Considering the source, that could be possible," I said.

"I give up," said John.

\#\#\#

Lloyd and I decided that it was time to find the bus driver from the 38 Geary bus. The best place to start would be the 38 Geary, of course. We started by getting on a bus, riding for a block, and then getting off at the next block. The bus drivers never took our transfers, and we found him on the fifth bus we tried this way.

We rode his bus all the way out to the end of the line. As the bus pulled up to rest, I looked out and saw a small statue guarding the ruins of a park across the street from a few squat houses. I remembered that Cathy had a thing for this statue of Diana the Hunter, and I felt my heart sigh as I remembered the last time I'd seen her The driver opened the door with a hiss and nimbly jumped outside. This got Lloyd's attention — he grabbed me and shook me into lucidity.

"Come on, man," said Lloyd.

I was here with Lloyd, near one of his hellish statues.

We moved down the stairs towards the driver. He had finished almost a quarter of his cigarette in the time it took us to get out of our seats and down the stairs. He looked up at us from behind the glowing ember as we stepped off of the bus, and slowly pulled in a lungful of smoke. We could tell he was trying to remember us.

"Crazy white boys. You were there the night of the vampire," he said.

"There's no such thing as vampires," I said.

"You say that then too," he said. "I think maybe you're right — from your point of view. A vampire isn't some guy with a funny accent in a cape. It's a zombie powered by human blood. It's an animal. So vampires like you know it don't exist. So that's the end of that, eh?"

"We're not here about that," I said.

The bus driver regarded us again. Lloyd stepped forward.

"We need your help," said Lloyd, looking about as compassionate as a Satanist could.

"What do you want with me? I'm a bus driver," he said, eying us.

"Don't jive me, I saw what you did with the sutras on that vampire," said Lloyd. "You're some kind of a monk."

"I pray sometimes," said the bus driver, warily. "You don't have to be a monk to do that."

"Yeah, well, you know some things we don't know," I said.

"Ha! You are getting smarter!" said the bus driver.

"What do you know about the statues in this city?" asked Lloyd.

"Depends on which ones," he said. "Are you talking about the ones that form the giant pentacle, or the ones that form a giant yin-yang symbol ?"

"What?" said Lloyd.

"I'm joking with you," said the bus driver, looking very serious.

"The pentacle," said Lloyd.

"I don't do western magic," said the bus driver.

"Come on, Lloyd," I said. "I need a walk. He's not going to help us."

"Here's our number," said Lloyd, handing the bus driver a card. "Call us."

The bus driver shrugged and took it.

###

When we got back to the house, John and Sam were engaged in scanning in pages of the book.

"What are you doing?" I asked.

Sam looked at me, then went back to scanning.

"I'm going to take each of these symbols and make a font out of it," she said.

"That's a lot of work," I said.

"Not me personally," she said. "I know this guy who does this for a living."

"What'll that do?" I asked.

"It'll make it so we can try and crack this thing on the computer," said John, as he clicked his way through the scanning program.

"We've had to figure out how many different characters there are," said Sam. "So far, we've only counted twenty-three."

Anyone who is familiar with numbers and with conspiracy theory will know that the number twenty-three occurs far too many times for comfort in everyday life. There is the number of chromosome pairs in human DNA (23), and so on and so on — this subject has been broached by far better thinkers than myself. Once again, coincidence conspired against us to reveal the nature of the problem we were up against.

"It's Latin," said Lloyd.

"Latin?" said John. "What do you mean, Latin? From what period? Later-period Latin had twenty-four letters, and I expect any garden-variety sorcerer would use the latest version, ya know?"

"These aren't garden-variety sorcerers," said Lloyd. "These guys were out to do something bad."

Lloyd was interrupted by a police car speeding in front of the house. It stole our attention by blurting out two short beeps over the cruiser's public address system. John got up quickly for a better view, and I turned on my pocket scanner to see what was going on.

The traffic on all the police channels was very hard to understand. This was because a lot of people were trying to talk at once, and the effect on the normal tidiness of radio traffic on the ancient repeater system San Francisco relies upon for police communications was devastating. Finally one person's voice broke through and stayed keyed on the repeater.

"We have an officer down, I repeat, officer down," said the manic voice, with gunfire in the background.

"Should we go look?" said Sam.

We all looked at her like she was insane.

"Lead poisoning kills a lot of people every year," said Lloyd. "I'd rather talk about Latin."

"Fine by me," said John.

"I third that," said I.

"What about Latin?" asked Sam.

"Latin from about the 1st century AD had only twenty-three letters," said

Lloyd.

"That's it?" said Sam.

"Well, I would assume it's some kind of really old spell," said Lloyd. "Something that can only be performed once every one or two thousand years"

"Well, why on the year 2000?" I asked. "Why not every one thousand years and the next year be 2380 or something?"

"Because you don't know shit about casting spells," said Lloyd. "Numbers are very much involved, and significant numbers are nodal points in the fabric of time and space. It stands to reason that with this being number 2000 in the year of our Lord Jesus Christ on a Popsicle Stick that the tensions of everyone noting the date and thinking it meant something might generate a huge amount of energy that could be used to drive some kind of cosmic reaction. I don't know, I just worship Satan. I leave magic to weirdos like that bus driver.

"You found him?" asked John.

"Yeah, we found him," I said. "He's not going to help us."

"Damn," said John.

"No big deal," I lied.

###

Sam had a lot of interesting people who came to her website. There's a saying among sex industry workers — the bigger the wallet, the bigger the kink. A lot of Silicon Valley executives, programmers, and real estate agents have very large wallets.

One of the people that came to her website, as she put it, was a redhot young programmer who worked in cryptography systems.

"I treat him special," said Sam.

"Define special."

"He's a friend of mine, a personal friend. I've known him for years. I used to babysit him."

"Say what?" I asked.

"I kinda let him do what he wants, because he's got half a million shares in the company he helps run. He's the brains behind it."

"What company is that?" I asked.

The answer was terrifying.

"Good god," I said. "He's worth a fortune."

"Yup," said Sam. "If he can't crack this code, nobody can."

Lloyd looked disgruntled. "Does he know Latin?"

"Come on, boys, we're taking a bus ride," said Sam, as she scooped up a disk that slid out of a drive on her computer. "We've got to get this to Barnabas."

"Barnabas?" I asked.

"It's his real name," said Sam. "His parents watched a lot of soap operas, he says."

###

Barnabas Rawlins looked like any other programmer I'd ever met. A long, tangled mess of frizzy brown hair framed a thin face that seemed to be pushed into his skull beginning at a point somewhere below the bridge of his thick eyeglasses. I met him outside a security door at the Embarcadero Center in San Francisco. Sam dragged us onto MUNI and into the subway to end up across from the ferry building in a large downtown mall under the office of the Barnabas' company. As we went through the doors into the elevator lobby, I looked down and out over a large park with a statue of Lady Justice right in the middle of it. I found myself thanking whatever gods of symbolism there might be that she was blindfolded. At least she wasn't moving.

15

Cracking the Code

T he lanky lad waved a passcard over a reader pad embedded in the wall with the ease of someone who had done it untold times before. He wasn't goth at all, but the pale skin was there. He wore a bright red athletic t-shirt and a large pair of baggy blue jeans that had twice as much fabric as needed in them. He seemed like a normal kid, except for one thing. His eyes were slightly magnified by his glasses for a truly disturbing effect, and his eyes seemed to be extremely expressive despite this annoying feature.

"Hi, I'm Bo," said the boy.

"Sam said your name was Barnabas," I said.

"I don't like that name, I go by Bo," he said quietly.

I shrugged. Lloyd sniffed. John shifted uneasily. Sam threw her arms around Bo.

"Bo here is such a sweetie," she gushed. "Bo, remember how you owed me a favor?"

Yet again, Sam was using her femininity to get something. I felt odd watching her use it on someone that it worked on. It usually failed on me and Lloyd and John because we lived with her, but it was obvious to me that the relationship Sam had with Bo was a little different than this. I remember having a crush on my first babysitter too.

"Yeah, I know," Bo said. He was a bit glum.

"Well, this one is important," she said. She pulled out the book and handed it to him as we walked into an office. It seemed a bit surreal -we were all dressed in old street clothes. This contrasted with the cherrywood paneling and sleek glass décor of the office. Everything behind the door screamed 'executive', except for the fact that there was little to no furniture, the walls were bare, and the room was dominated by a huge glass desk with a nondescript computer on it. Like all good geeks, Bo had built his own computer. He sat at the desk with the book and opened it.

As books go, this one was fairly uninteresting except that it was obviously old. The cover was stained musty leather, covered with discolorations. There was nothing to identify the contents of the book, and as Bo opened it, he did the exact same thing I always do with books that are obviously old — he leaned his head in deeply and breathed in the dry heavy paper smell of old book.

"Wow, acid-free paper," he said.

"Can you tell what it says?" asked Sam, eagerly.

"Yes, I am scanning it with my retinal implants right now," he said dourly. Lloyd chuckled.

"I think it's Latin," he said.

Bo looked up.

"Why do you say that?" he asked.

"Because it only has twenty-three letters," said Lloyd.

"Latin has twenty-four letters," said Bo.

"First century Latin had twenty-three letters," said Lloyd. "I think some of the things in this book might be copied from that time period.

"Wow, someone who knows what they're talking about," said Bo dryly.

"I'm gonna go smoke a cigarette," said Lloyd, turning suddenly and walking out the door.

"Me too," said John, and he ran after Lloyd.

Bo had little to no social skills. I found myself shifting, embarrassed, as he talked to Sam about codebreaking and substitution ciphers. He totally ignored me and talked straight to Sam unless he was spoken to. When he did talk, I felt like he was looking down at me even though he was sitting and I was standing. It started to irritate me, and I wished that I smoked as well. After Sam gave Bo the disk with the font she had made from the symbols in the book, Bo talked with Sam about how long it would take him to do this project.

"Three months," he said.

"You've got to be kidding me," she said. "That's after the first of the year."

"I can't do it before then, we've got a major project and I'm slammed." he said.

"I thought you had all the crypto stuff at your disposal," she said.

"I'll see what I can do. Call me back tomorrow," he said.

"Fine," Sam said. She turned on her heel and walked out. "Come on, Derwood."

Grumbling, I followed her. After I left the building, I realized that I'd never seen Lloyd smoke anything other than marijuana.

###

"Goddamn, what a prick," said Lloyd. "You had a hand in shaping that miscreant? No wonder he's fucked in the head."

"Shut up, Lloyd," said Sam. She looked pissed.

"What's eating you?" I asked.

"I just wanna find out what's in that book," she said.

We walked out of the Embarcadero center and made our way down Battery Street to Market Street. The Financial District of San Francisco was deserted, this being a Sunday. As we got to Market Street, we saw a 21 Hayes bus sitting at the bus stop waiting, and a familiar, wiry Chinese man smoking a cigarette outside the bus.

"Great, our driver is Wong Fei Hong again," said Lloyd.The reference was totally lost on me.

The bus driver looked up at us through a cloud of smoke from his rapidly diminishing fag. He grinned a big grin that was all steel dental work and dark stains and looked like he was about to say something when it happened.

The ground began to shake.

Most people think Californians are totally insane to live with earthquakes. The truth of the matter is that most earthquakes are small ones that you barely feel. Anything below a four on the Richter scale is barely even worth mentioning. As I've said before, I grew up in Georgia. Every single day during the summer, we would get these huge thunderstorms that rolled across the piedmont of the state, bringing rain, lightning and occasionally tornadoes to terrified people. During the late summer and fall, hurricanes would lash angrily at the coast. A small earthquake every three or four months is a fairly good deal, in my book. I used to have a theory that you could tell everything you needed to know about a place by picking up a local phone book and seeing what disasters they warned you about in the front. In Georgia, it was tornadoes. In Louisiana, it was hurricanes. In Seattle, it was volcanoes. I'll take my chances with the ground shaking, thank you very much.

This was definitely not a 4.0 on the Richter scale. It started out as a low rumble, as if a heavy truck with tires made out of square blocks of rock were driving by. Instead of dying off in a few seconds, like most good earthquakes, the ground kept jiggling under our feet, and we looked at each other wondering what was going on for a second before realization hit us.

Ten seconds after the initial rumbling had begun, the ground shook even more violently and then started to calm down. We looked up at the swaying skyscrapers of the Financial District, and for a second I imagined one of them falling and starting a chain reaction. These buildings are going to be like God's own dominoes, I thought.

The vibrations came to a stop, the rumbling ceased, and we were left standing on the sidewalk in a creepy silence that was only broken by a cacophony of car alarms coming from all directions.

"Wow, creepy white kids again," said the bus driver. "You guys always bring trouble, you know that?"

"Yeah, we're all psychos with guns," I replied.

"I heard that too," said the bus driver. "You don't look the type."

"What exactly is 'The Type'?" asked Lloyd.

"You have to be waving a gun around, first off," said the bus driver.

94

"Don't tempt me," said Lloyd under his breath.

"When are you leaving?" asked John.

"Right now," said the bus driver, flicking his smoldering butt into the gutter and turning towards the bus.

"Let's go," I said, looking at the sky nervously. I was waiting for the real earthquake.

###

In violation of all MUNI rules, the bus driver talked to us the entire way home. He was a small, wiry man, with his hair clinging to his skull in a bowl cut. He was short compared to me, about five feet three inches by my guess. He chattered at my friends while I used an earphone to try and figure out what band MUNI transmitted their driver instructions on -the bus had a built-in radio and I was scanning for a signal that matched the squawking tones coming from the box next to his seat. The scanner moved over hundreds of signals while the man chattered at my friends.

"My name's Charlie," he said. "Charlie Lee. What's your names?"

"Lloyd Stark," said Lloyd.

"John Cooper," said John.

"Samantha Strange," said Sam.

"People have weird names in this town," said Charlie Lee.

SQUAWK. Wrong frequency.

"You guys still going on about that pentacle thing?" asked the bus driver.

"This is the bus driver you guys were telling me about," said Sam. Realization was just starting to hit her.

"They tell you about the hopping vampire, too?" asked Charlie.

"Um, no," said Sam.

"That's OK, I send it back to the Hell it came from," he said.

"The hell it came from?" asked John.

"Chinese people have a lot of hells," said Lloyd.

"You are right!" exclaimed Charlie. "There are three ways to suffer after death — Hell, hungry demons, or the state of brutes. Most people just go to

95

one of the Hells."

"What kind of Hells are there?" I asked, looking up from my radio for a second. There was still no match on the squawking tones through my earpiece.

"Well, there's actually one overriding afterlife," said Charlie. "There are ten kings of Hell, and they have a hell for almost any punishment imaginable. For example, if you lived your life killing flies, you would be condemned to the Hell of the Smothering Maggots."

"Oh, gross," said Sam.

"We already live in Hell," said Lloyd.

"'All Hells in this world are the prisons you make in your heart; all battles must be fought there,'" said Charlie. "My grandma used to say that to me."

"Your grandmother sounds wise," I said. I twirled a dial on my radio, trying to find the ear-piercing tones.

"So what do you think is happening with the pentacle?" asked Lloyd.

"Buncha crazy white guys," said Charlie. "There's no way just drawing out a big star in statues is gonna destroy this town."

"Doesn't it make you curious?" asked Lloyd.

"Not really."

"Haven't you noticed a lot more weird stuff happening lately?" Lloyd pressed Charlie further.

Charlie paused a second.

"Things have been a little busy lately," he said finally. "The buses are later than ever."

"So what kind of Hell do you think they were trying to open up?" Sam asked.

"White man's Hell," said Charlie. "The one that doesn't exist."

Lloyd snorted again.

SQUAWK. Bingo. I found the frequency at that moment.

We pulled up to our stop and said our goodbyes to Charlie Lee.

"Please call us," I said. "We need help with what we're trying to do."

"I will think about it," said Charlie Lee.

"We only have until December 31st," said Lloyd.

"End of the world? Cool," said Charlie.

"End of this city, maybe," said John.

Charlie looked at him.

"I will think about it," he announced. "In the meantime, you guys should check your house for earthquake damage."

"Thank you," I said. "Keep in touch."

###

We trudged back to our house, where we found the only damage was a fallen bookshelf. I reminded myself to get anchors for the bookcases as I sat in the living room and doodled Latin numerals on a piece of paper while listening to MUNI transmissions. Lloyd and Sam went to their respective rooms, and John sat down on the couch next to me.

"What's up?" said John, producing a small bag and a rolling paper. He started rolling a smelly joint without looking at his hands.

"I'm listening to MUNI," I said. I pulled the earpiece out of the radio and let John listen in to the leaden MUNI control operator blandly relaying instructions.

"Cool," he said. "What for?"

"I don't know," I said. "But I'm going to see if there's a pattern to the weird shit Charlie said is happening on MUNI."

"And what if there is a pattern?" asked John, lighting the joint and puffing on it before handing it to me.

"I'm thinking about that," I said.

John and I sat on the couch, silently passing the joint between us while waiting for any word from Barnabas.

16

Bay City Rollers

Bo has found something," announced Sam about two weeks after we had met him. It was noon on a Saturday, and we were standing in the living room when she rushed in with her proclamation.

The news was welcome. The days between then and now had been filled with further attempts to get in touch with Charlie Lee. We were reduced to playing phone tag with the manic little man, leaving recorded pleas on his answering machine that had no English on the outgoing message.

"When can we get it?" asked Lloyd. He was anxious to start reading the Latin inscriptions — I suspected he wanted to copy some of the formulary down for his own use.

"Tonight," said Sam. "Barnabas darling wants us to meet him at seven PM."

"Won't work for me," said John.

"We don't need you," said Sam. "Bo wants us to meet him at his house, before he goes out."

"I have some extra work to do," said John. "I told them I'd help out tonight."

"Creepy, dude," said Lloyd, as he shifted his weight to direct himself out of the living room. "Have fun with your stiffies."

###

At three PM I tried Charlie Lee for what I swore would be the last time. I'd

98

had enough of the phone messages and his tendency to not return calls. I was about to hang up on the machine when suddenly the line came alive with the sound of Charlie's voice saying something in Chinese.

"Charlie Lee?" I asked.

"Ya, you got it," said the tinny voice emanating from the earpiece.

"This is the crazy white kid from the bus," I said. "You know, the…"

"Ya, I remember you," he said. "I keep thinking I want to talk to you."

"Should we meet?" I asked.

"Of course we should meet, you crazy white boy." he said. "I can't tell you over the phone."

"When do you want to meet?" I asked.

"What are you doing at six PM tonight?" he asked.

"I have plans at seven PM," I said. "But you might be interested in those plans."

"Oh yah?" asked Charlie. "What's up?"

"We found a book in our house that we are having translated," I started. "We think it might have something to do with all the strange things happening in this town lately."

"No shit?" he asked. "Is it in Chinese?"

"No, it's in Latin," I said.

"Ha," said Charlie. "I'll meet you at six-thirty and we'll go see this book then."

"OK," I said, wondering what else was up. "Where should we meet you?"

We met Charlie Lee at a small dessert shop in Chinatown that sat between a gaudy tourist bauble shop on the corner and a storefront that offered a wide variety of gnarled roots for purchase. I watched Lloyd haggle with the shop owner over a strange dried mushroom, finally buying it for a few pennies. Charlie grunted as he saw Lloyd and his dried mushroom, smiling quietly to himself.

We walked down Grant Street towards North Beach. Barnabas lived in a large apartment in North Beach, and we moved along for several blocks watching store windows flash past. Every window in Chinatown seems to have a more surprising sight than the last. I thought I'd never see anything weirder than a plastic bin of tiny live frogs until I saw a candy that looked like a centipede dipped in caramel hanging in one window. As we reached the end of Chinatown, Sam pointed us towards Broadway. The street was alive with women calling to us from the strip joints, informing us that they specialized in couples and group shows. A gaggle of young Asian men stood outside a video game parlor, with nylon windbreakers barely hiding the outline of gun butts nestled on their hips. I saw a nightclub that had once housed a rather popular goth/industrial club — in the wake of the shootings, any club night with the words 'gothic' or 'industrial' had been quickly shut down.

We arrived at Bo's house at seven PM sharp. Bo did not.

We waited.

And waited.

And waited.

At eight, we decided to get something to eat.

We walked back through the gauntlet of strippers, sex stores, and young hoodlums toward Grant Street. There was an insidious chain hamburger restaurant on the corner called 'Lil Cole's Shakes and Burgers'. We could order a patty of soybean enhanced meat byproduct on a soyflour bun for fifty-five cents. Sam and I stayed outside while Lloyd and Charlie walked in to get a drink and a small burger to go.

From the depths of Sam's purse, something started playing 'Toccata in Fugue'. I looked at Sam, and she looked at her handbag.

"Oh shit, my cell phone," said Sam. "I almost forgot I had one."

"I didn't know you had one," I said.

"Someone gave it to me," said Sam. She pulled out a small device, smoothly pulled an antenna out of it, and unfolded it.

"Hello?" she shouted into it.

Phone conversations that include only half of the conversation leave a little to be desired. In my case, it was wholly unsatisfying — Sam answered back and forth with various versions of 'uh huh' and 'yeah'. I was able to deduce that she was indeed talking to Barnabas. I resolved to call him Barnabas now, after he'd left us sitting outside his apartment on a November San Francisco evening. I decided I would even call him Barnabas to his face when I saw him next.

"OK," said Sam. "They aren't going to like that."

"Aren't going to like what?" I asked, as Sam put her hand up in a motion to quiet me.

"Uh huh," she repeated. She whipped out a pen and scribbled on the back of her hand.

"OK," she said. "I'll see you in a bit."

She pulled the phone away from her head and punched a button on it.

"Well," I asked, as Lloyd and Charlie came walking out with a cup of liquid and a small breaded hockey puck in each hand.

"Fucking kids," spat Sam.

"What?" I asked.

"We have to go meet him," said Sam. "Some of his friends talked him into going somewhere."

"What?" asked Lloyd. "What'd I miss?"

"We been sitting here for nothing," said Charlie. "Well, I got me a burger."

"Where do we have to go?" I asked Sam.

"To South of Market," she said. "We need to hop a 15 Third. Luckily, we're at a corner where one stops."

"Great," said Lloyd. "What is this now?"

"It's some company down there that Bo knows," said Sam. "They're some kind of user interface design house, and they are throwing a party. A rave."

"A party?" asked Charlie. "I like parties."

"A rave," I said. "Bo is dragging us to a rave."

"Yeah," said Sam. "Techno mother fucker."

###

The 15 Third deposited us in front of a large warehouse building that seemed to vibrate from within. One of the floors swirled with multicolored lights, and we heard a lot of bass coming from above our heads.

"Can we just stay down here?" I asked. I looked around the street.

The warehouse was at the end of a small alley. Further down the alley, I saw the spaces widen out into a large, dimly-lit park. I tried to concentrate on the filling station on the other corner of the alley, but it was no good — I had already noticed the statue that stood with its right arm outstretched, deep in the shadows of the park.

"Shit," I muttered.

"What?" asked Sam.

I pointed down the alley and heard a grunt from Lloyd.

"You folks are scared of every little shadow," said Charlie. "I wanna see this party."

"It's a rave," said Sam.

We walked in and were greeted by a large musclebound man in a black t-shirt and Lycra pants. I looked him up and down while he checked the guest list for our names. A few guys came wandering out of a stairwell towards the back, giggling and slapping each other on the back.

"Go ahead," said the slab of beef monitoring the door list. "You're on there. Up the stairs."

Charlie froze as we walked towards the stairs.

"We need to leave," he said.

"What?" said Sam.

"Now!" Charlie shouted, and he started to sprint towards the door.

"What the fuck?" said Lloyd, and then he was sprinting too.

Sam and I started at the same time, and we had no sooner made it through the front door of the building than a low rumble started to rattle our teeth.

It was too violent to be an aftershock. We stumbled into the alley next door and were nearly thrown from our feet by the rolling street. This was a full-fledged temblor, and we pitched around on the tarmac for a good fifty or sixty seconds. Bricks flew from buildings, and I watched in horror as the warehouse swayed sickeningly. Visions of our translated text buried under mounds of rubble filled my head as I saw the first people spill into the streets from the warehouse.

The buildings shuddered to a stop and telephone poles slowly halted their rocking as the rumbling noise was replaced with the sound of hundreds of car alarms and distant screaming.

It was only after about five seconds that we realized that the screaming wasn't so distant.

Sam was racing towards the warehouse before any of us could gather ourselves. The lights flickered and went out all around us — we heard explosions in the distance. I noticed that the slab of beef working the door had run into the street, but was moving back inside very quickly. As he opened the cracked glass door, the volume of the screaming increased a hundredfold.

Something was happening inside the warehouse.

The entire structure strobed with arcing current and a bright light appeared on the roof as we ran for the front door. What greeted us was a shocking sight — hundreds of panicked South of Market scenesters had run for the doors when the earthquake had started, and hundreds more behind them had fallen on them when they had tripped with the rolling motion of the floor. The panic increased, until a large mass of hallucinating twenty-year-olds had filled the stairwell. What lay before us, in what Charlie jokingly referred to later as the Chinese 'Hell of Being Dressed Very Badly For Death', were about three hundred screaming, bleeding, suffocating, crying and shitting people dressed in giant pants. Glowsticks made the scene even more surreal as we caught glimpses of suffering in the pale luminescence — jutting bone and da-glo illuminations of spurting blood.

"Oh, shit," said Lloyd, and he looked away.

"Sam!" I yelled. "See if your cell phone still works."

Charlie and Lloyd started towards the stairwell as Sam grabbed for her purse and punched buttons.

"Shit, it's dead!" she screamed and suddenly a strobe of light flashed across the stairwell. I saw a familiar face beneath a crush of bodies and my blood ran cold.

"Sam, go find a fire box!" I yelled. "Pull the lever on it!"

San Francisco has the oldest system of fire alarm boxes in the world. Installed after the 1906 earthquake, the boxes were extremely simple — a single wire connected the box to the main San Francisco Fire Department on McAllister Street near City Hall. When the level was pulled, a wind-up spring spun a disk that connected to the wire. This disk had holes punched in it that corresponded to the number of the fire box - - when it went off, a light would light up at the central office on a map showing all of the fireboxes in the city.The system worked perfectly during the 1989 earthquake, and I sent Sam after one of these boxes, hoping that she wouldn't see her friend's lifeless body crushed beneath a few thousand pounds of screaming kids on drugs. Sam ran towards the corner without looking at the stairs.

I ran to where Barnabas was protruding from beneath the pile, and got there as Lloyd was helping a person with a broken leg from off the top of the pile.

"He's dead," said Lloyd, grunting as he tried to pull the screaming girl off of her broken leg. Arms reached at us from the flicking darkness, and the glowsticks wouldn't go out. I had read about scenes like this in Dante.

"We have to get him out of there!" I said.

"No we don't," said Lloyd, as he held up a flat piece of plastic about three inches square. I recognized it as a proprietary-format high-density storage disk.

"I can read this on my computer at home."

\#\#\#

Sam and I sat, hunkering on the curb in the alley, watching the rescue operations. I held her as they pulled the tangled bodies away from the stampeded stairwell. Lloyd and Charlie helped pull people out until about three in the morning, when they stumbled out to find us huddled under a fire department blanket. We stood up and looked around at the blackened city looming ahead of us, and watched the fire engines strobing the tiny park in the alleyway with their red lights.

With its right hand pointing downward, the statue in the little park stared impassively at us as we turned towards the sound of fire engines and car alarms in the distance and started the long walk home.

17

Manus Glorificus

We walked up Third Street towards Market Street from the disaster area. Sam cried into my shoulder most of the way. Lloyd and Charlie were silent. Sirens and darkness and car horns permeated the night air. The only light was from the cars that occasionally drove by.

"This sucks," said Charlie. "Let's find a cab."

"Yeah," said Lloyd. "I have flat feet."

I had to admit, they had a point. Finding a cab would probably be a little hard under the circumstances. I felt obligated to point this out.

"How much money do we have?" I asked. "I only have a five."

"I have a twenty," said Charlie.

"I have enough," said Lloyd. "I'll cover it."

A voice from the shadows spoke up.

"I was gonna go looting, but now I can get me some cash," it said. "Don't move or I'll fucking shoot you."

I watched Lloyd. I knew he usually carried his gun, but he froze along with all of us. Sam hugged me even tighter and I found my blood frozen. People didn't normally go around robbing people when the power went out in San Francisco — this guy must have been from out of town or something.

"Turn around slowly and keep your hands where I can seen them," said the voice.

We turned. Charlie was on my left side, Sam was on my right, and Lloyd was beyond her. I heard the man approach Charlie and quietly swore — we were in Lloyd's line of fire.

"You must be grade A idiot, boy," said Charlie.

"Shut your fucking mouth, chink," said the voice as it moved closer to us. He must have been watching us for a while before trying to rob us.

"I say what I want," said Charlie. I heard a rush of wind and I caught a movement out of the corner of my left eye. I turned my head involuntarily.

In the time it took me to turn my head, Charlie had grabbed the man's hand and pointed the gun upwards. A shot went off, and then I heard several meaty thuds. In the dim light, I watched in astonishment. Charlie kicked the man five times in the stomach, broke his shoulder, and then, using the elbow that wasn't engaged in holding the gun upwards, he drove the man's face into his knee. The man crumpled.

Within three seconds it was over.

"Holy fuck!" I exclaimed.

"Wow," said Lloyd.

Sam was silent.

"Stupid people," said Charlie, and then a shot rang out.

The muzzle flash illuminated an alley we had overlooked. I heard the bullet whiz by our ears and Lloyd dove for the relative safety of a doorwell. I tried to hustle Sam to the doorwell too, but I was slowed by my attempts to watch what happened next.

Charlie zig-zagged across the street towards the alley. Another shot rang out, and I saw the pimply kid holding the gun trying to hit Charlie. Then Charlie was on him. The gun was knocked clear of the kid's hand, and Charlie yanked the kid into the street while kicking him in the head as he flew past. Charlie landed in a ready stance and looked around as the boy collapsed on his comatose friend.

"Crazy people tonight," said Charlie. "Earthquake shake their brain loose."

"Gimme one of those guns," said Sam.

Charlie walked over, grabbed one of the guns from the pavement, and tossed it onto the roof of a nearby building.

"Guns can kill people," he said.

"Evidently, so can you," sneered Lloyd, walking out of the doorwell.

Charlie picked up the other gun and tossed it onto the roof as well.

"I can control myself," said Charlie. "Once the bullet leaves the barrel, nobody can undo what it does."

"You've got a point," said Lloyd. "Where'd you learn those moves?"

"Please," said Charlie. "I grew up as youngest of six boys. I had to learn to defend myself."

Lloyd almost laughed. "So you learned the choppy socky for when your older brothers took turns beating on you?"

"They almost never took turns," said Charlie quietly as a taxicab turned the corner, stopping to avoid the bodies in the street. I looked over at Charlie, and remembered why we'd gone to meet him in the first place.

"Weren't you going to tell me something, Charlie?" I asked.

"Was I?" he said. "No, I just wanted to talk to you wackos again. See what I get for being nice? I get shot at."

###

"Some night, eh?" asked the taxicab driver.

"Yeah, it was," I said. I sat between Sam and Lloyd, and Charlie took shotgun.

"Lotta people hurt tonight, I hear," said the cabbie. "A building collapsed in the Marina District, and there was a bunch of people in the restaurant in the bottom floor. I hear there's still a fire going on down there."

"Fuck," I said quietly.

"Yeah," said the cabbie. "Fuck."

"Anywhere else?" said Charlie. "How is Chinatown?"

"Chinatown's a mess, man," said the cabbie. "I'd stay outta there if you can."

Charlie looked at me.

"Yeah, you can stay with us, man," said Lloyd. "We have an extra room."

"Just tonight," I said.

Sam was asleep. We told the driver to head to our neighborhood, which he said had survived the earthquake relatively unscathed.

\#\#\#

The house was intact, but the contents were a mess. The coatrack in the foyer that Sam had brought with her had fallen down and we had to push past a morass of coats to get the door open. One of the pictures we had hung up using the decorative molding near the ceiling had flipped completely over and now faced the wall. In the living room, the television had fallen out of the entertainment center and shattered on the floor, while all the knick-knacks on the mantelpiece lay strewn across the floor.

"Is that you guys?" called a voice from upstairs that belonged to John.

"Yes, it's us," I called out. "We have a houseguest."

"Coming down!" shouted John, as a flashlight bounced around the walls of the staircase and showed us the mad descent of our crotchtouching roommate.

John had spent most of the night cleaning the mess that the kitchen was in. He had then started in on his room. Luckily, we had bolted all of the bookcases to the walls and the cabinets all had lips on their shelves.

"We didn't lose any dishes, but I think the ones in the dish drainer are a goner," said John.

"How's your room?" I asked.

"What's that smell?" asked Sam.

"You people got a body in here?" asked Charlie.

I suddenly detected a faint chemical smell, and realized it came from John.

"Jesus, John, wash that formaldehyde shit off of you," I said. "That causes cancer in lab animals."

"So does life," said John. "It was just a small accident at work. We contained it."

I suddenly got wary. A large copper vat of formaldehyde springing a leak was not a laughing matter.

"How small?" I asked.

"I dropped a jar," he said, a bit nervously.

"Ewwww," said Lloyd and I, almost simultaneously.

"Yeah, it was gross," he said, and he looked a bit more nervous. I grew suspicious.

"What did you bring home?" I asked. At this, John looked very nervous.

"Nothing!" he protested.

Before John could protest further, I ran up the stairs.

Lloyd, Sam, and Charlie looked at each other in bewilderment and slow shock as the thought "There's human body parts here the landlord didn't bring into this house" cascaded through their minds. I had a good ten feet on John and easily got to his door before he did. A strange light sputtered and crackled on the other side of his door, and the evidence presented itself in the crack at the base of the portal. I grabbed the knob and turned.

In the middle of the floor stood a severed hand on its wrist. A single flame at the tip of each of the fingers illuminated the surface of the hand. Only the thumb was unlit. The skin had a strange complexion and as I looked at it, I realized that it was covered in fat and wax. It sat upon one end of a small board, and the flames guttered maliciously at the intrusion of air the open door presented. Dribbles of wax ran down its surface, and bones protruded from the tips of the fingers and blackened. I stared in shock as John ran into my back.

"What the fuck is that?"

"Um," began John. "I think I'd better explain some things to you and apologize."

I heard the stairs creak and the others were behind John, looking at me standing next to the horror on the floor.

"Apologize for what?" asked Lloyd. "You're more core than I am, dude.You made a Hand of Glory."

###

Over the course of the next two hours of interrogation, the guilty party related the entire story of how he had cracked the code of the book without the help of computers or scanning software. Lloyd fiddled with the wasted time represented by the plastic disk he held, and I got kind of scared of the possibility that John have far more intelligence than he put into practice in his everyday life.

"The dude who made that book was a little too meticulous, if you know what I mean," he said.

"What do you mean?" I asked.

"He means that the book's writer did a little recurring pattern in the book that enabled him to crack the code, Derwood," said Lloyd.

Lloyd looked smug, and if Sam's friend hadn't lost his life he might have said something aloud about how some human brains could be better than computers and socially inept nerds combined. Thankfully, he didn't. I looked back at John to see his response.

"Lloyd's right," said John. "The guy was psycho. You know what he did? He numbered his pages. In Latin. Then he encrypted the page numbers. What a fucking idiot."

"Wow," said Sam. "That is stupid."

John produced a single sheet of ruled notebook paper with a number and a title across the top.

It said: I. Manus Glorificus.

"I have the entire cipher here, and I was going to do the rest of the book," he said. "But this was the first one I did, and I had to try the recipe out."

"That's weak," I said.

"Human beings are weak that way," said Lloyd. "It won't work unless you light the thumb, man."

"What does it do?" I asked.

"I don't know," said John.

Lloyd snickered.

"This is so typical," said Lloyd. "This here is an infamous magical talisman and you just whipped one up."

"I got all the ingredients!" said John.

Lloyd snatched the piece of paper and held it close to his thick horn-rimmed glasses.

"This doesn't say anything that I'd ever heard for a Hand of Glory," said

Lloyd. "It just says a hand, not the hand of a condemned murderer hanged and collected at midnight on a full moon."

"Maybe that was a lot of bullshit," I said.

Lloyd looked at me.

"Well, I dunno," he proclaimed. "Maybe it was, but why would this guy have a recipe for this in his book as the first recipe? That's a pretty core talisman."

"What does it do?" asked Charlie. He appeared very interested in the sputtering piece of human meat on the floor.

"It's a thieving tool," said Lloyd. "A robber carries one of these. Anyone who isn't touching that board in some way falls asleep, for about fifty feet around the thing. It's a weird kind of spell and good-luck-in-thievery charm all rolled into one."

"Cool," said John.

"Put it out," I said.

John obeyed, looking like a scolded puppy dog.

"OK, I think the time has come where we have to make a few promises to each other," I started.

"Hey, man," said Lloyd. "It's every man for himself in this stupid world."

"No, listen to him," said Sam.

"You too, John," I said. "If we don't start telling each other as soon as we find things out, we're never going to be able to beat this thing."

"I don't see why," said John. "I want to be the one to save the world."

"That's not the point," I said. "The point is that unless we work together, we might blow the entire thing. Do you want that?"

"No," said John.

"No," said Lloyd.

I looked at Charlie and Sam. They smiled, and I knew instantly that they understood where I was coming from.

"Now that we all know what we're going to be aiming for, let's finish this thing," I said. "I for one don't want any of the deaths we've seen since this bullshit started to be in vain, and I hope you don't either."

"Amen," said Sam.

We stood in a circle as lazy curls of smoke drifted upward from the charred fingertips of the wax-encrusted hand.

18

Haircut 2000

I awoke to the sound of the telephone ringing at about two PM. I opened my eyes slightly and debated letting the machine get it, and then the sudden realization that the phones were working made me nearly fall out of bed trying to grab at the receiver.

"Hello?" I asked.

"Hey honey!" wafted a chipper voice over the line.

Was this Cathy?

"Cathy?" I asked.

"Of course it is, my love," said Cathy, her voice turned hollow and tinny by a bad phone line.

"Jesus, I've missed you," I said enthusiastically.

"I've missed you too, hon," she said. "I've been trying to call ever since last night — the quake was all over the news."

"What in our lives hasn't been all over the news lately?" I asked.

Cathy laughed. I never thought I'd hear her laugh this soon.

"How's the house?" she asked.

"It's fine, it's a good solid house," I said. "We lost some knick-knacks."

"How about everyone else?" she asked.

"Up for debate," I said. "Sam lost a good friend and we were there when it happened."

"Oh, shit," said Cathy. "Is she OK?"

"I don't know," I said. "She's a tough one, but I'm not sure how she's going to hold out with this one."

I explained the entire sordid situation with the rave and Barnabas.

"Give her my love, and if she needs anything, help her out," she said. "What were you doing at a rave?"

"How are you doing?" I asked.

"I want to come home," she said.

"What does the doctor think?" I asked.

"He thinks it's fine. Actually, he's insisting that I go," she said.

"Why's that?" I asked.

"I think I depressed him," she said.

"What?" I asked.

"Well, he seems to think that my knowledge of Hollywood gravesites is disturbing," she said.

Cathy had a slight obsession. She had a notebook of celebrity graves — people she thought were important. When she visited a grave, she'd mark it in her little book with the date and, if possible, a picture. She recounted to me how she'd stood in front of Valentino's crypt and left a pair of lipstick marks on the marble, stained pink by decades of similar homages. She saw the urn that held Peter Lorre's ashes. She visited the memorial to Douglas Fairbanks and stood at Bela Lugosi's crypt, trying to imagine the bones wrapped in the cape of Dracula. Evidently, the doctor found this all rather disturbing. I considered it a normal part of life with Cathy. She was even planning a trip to England to see Boris -Karloff's grave.

"I hate Los Angeles," she said. "I want to come home this weekend."

I thought about this.

"OK, that's fine," I said. "But when you get here, we have to talk about a few things."

"Like what?" she asked.

"Well, that's what we're trying to figure out," I said. "It's about all of us in the house, actually — it concerns us all."

"Oh, a house meeting," said Cathy. "Is Lloyd not flushing again?"

"Let's just save it, OK?"

###

Knocks on my door about five minutes after hanging up with Cathy made me wake up again. I put on a robe and surveyed the damage to our rooms as I answered the door.

"Who is it?" I asked — it could only be one of four people.

"This is Sam," said a surprisingly chipper voice. "Is your phone working?"

"Yeah, you need to use it?" I asked.

"Yeah, I do," she said as I opened the door. "I'll only be about five minutes, I'm going to check on some people and then I'm going to do my hair."

"Do it?" I asked.

"Yeah, you want a haircut?" she asked.

I decided that a new hairstyle was what I needed.

"Fuck, yeah," I said. "I need to do something cool for my last haircut of the millennium."

"Rock on," said Sam. "I was thinking of something a little more radical myself. Meet me in the kitchen in twenty minutes."

I listened as she walked away, and then I decided that I needed something a bit more radical as well. Our rooms were a mess, but not really anything that couldn't be handled in a few minutes. The bookcases were all bolted to the walls, but our chest of drawers had fallen forward onto the drawers. I picked it up while trying to find something to wear, and the drawers slid out. Earthquakes have a funny way of depositing things in such a way that everything will fall out if you pick it up. I cursed softly and picked out something to wear from the pile on the ground.

I laid out some grungy clothes on the queen-sized sled bed Cathy had bought, and looked at our walls to try and assess the damage. The only real problem was Cathy's collection of manacles, floggers and interesting toys that she had displayed on the wall near our bed — they were on a wooden rack that was held on the wall by nails, and the shaking had ripped the nails out of the wall. I saw a few days ahead of me trying to reattach the rack to the wall and cover the unsightly holes with spackle. I sighed and pulled an old shirt over my head.

116

Once I was dressed, I quickly shoved the clothes back into their drawers and picked up the old Underwood typewriter that had fallen on the floor from the top of the chest of drawers. It was a solid piece of steel from the 1920's, and didn't work — the fall to the floor hadn't damaged it in the slightest. I flicked the light a couple of times and made sure the electricity still worked. The power had come back on that morning. I decided to see what was up in the kitchen.

The smell of formaldehyde still permeated the hallway, and I looked warily at John's door. We had all gotten to bed about six in the morning, and I was quite sure that everyone was still asleep. The formaldehyde aroma was slowly being replaced with the rich smell of chicory coffee that Sam loved so much. I looked over the railing to the first floor of the house, and heard movement in the kitchen.

I came off the stairs into the kitchen to find Sam with tin foil on her hair and a plastic bag on top of that. I had never seen her bleach her hair before, and I wasn't exactly sure how it was done.

"What're ya doing?" I asked, pulling a cup out of the cupboard and moving towards the coffeepot.

"Bleaching," she said, around a mouthful of muffin. "I'm sick of straight black."

"I am too, sort of," I said.

"Then you need a bleach job too," she said. She moved towards me and I backed up.

"Whoa there," I said. "I only said 'sort of '."

"Well, what do you want done?" she asked.

"I wanna shave the sides again," I said, indicating the three inches of half-inch-long hair on the sides of my head, "but I want to keep the length on top and I want to make it two colors — I want to bleach stripes an inch wide on either side, color the middle part blue-black, and make the bleached parts purple."

"Wow," said Sam. "That's pretty radical for you."

"What are you doing?" I asked.

"Bleaching it out, and cutting it really short."

"That's pretty different for you as well," I said, remembering Sam's gloomy black rat's nest and inwardly crying over its loss. I liked Sam's hair the way it was.

"I do this sometimes," said Sam. "Like when I'm stressed out."

"Don't we all," I replied.

"You're going to be first with the clippers," she said as she moved towards me.

I sat down in a chair, and Sam took out a white sheet. She tied it tightly around my neck and arranged it so that it covered my entire body.

"Cathy called this morning," I said while Sam was prepping me.

"Oh yeah? How is she?" Sam asked.

"She's fine," I said. "I think the doctor has more to worry about than Cathy. He got very disturbed by her grave diary."

I took a moment to explain the grave diary to Sam. Sam listened, and as she moved away I saw her wipe a tear away.

"I'm sorry, Sam," I said. "I know death is a touchy subject right now."

"Well, why isn't it touchy for you?" she asked. I could see the tears welling up in her eyes.

"It's probably because nobody I care about has died yet," I replied. "I know it's going to happen — I was kind of scared when the guy in the nightclub was standing right over us. Nobody I know personally has died yet, though. I don't see it as a bad thing, either. Death is something natural, it's as easy as being born. Grief is for the people that live, though. I personally think that someone who has died is better off than we are, so I'm not sure if I'd cry that much. I'd be upset that I'd never get to talk to them ever again, but I wouldn't feel bad for them. I'd feel bad for me, and ultimately that's what grief is all about. It's rather selfish but necessary."

"I never really thought of it that way," said Sam.

"Well, I'm probably wrong," I said. "There are thousands of ways to think about it, maybe millions. I tend to agree with Lloyd when he says 'We already live in Hell'. I'm not sure there's anything that happens to your consciousness when you die. I just know that I don't like seeing people in pain, and I sometimes vacillate between wishing everyone would die, and wishing everyone would just be happy."

The razor clicked on and buzzed.

"Well, now some hair is gonna die," said Sam.

"Hair's already dead," I said as she dragged the buzzing tool across the side of my head. I felt hair fall away and hit the sheet on my shoulder.

"Good morning," said Lloyd, as he walked into the kitchen. "Hair cutting time, I see."

The razor snapped off.

"Yeah, you wanna be next?" asked Sam.

"No, I believe in hanging onto my life as long as possible," said Lloyd. "I haven't cut my hair in seven years."

We both stared at Lloyd in disbelief.

"Why is it only at your shoulders?" I asked.

"Because my hair is all brittle and shit, man," he said. "I comb it and it breaks off at about my shoulders. It might have something to do with me using regular hand soap all over my body, but I dunno. My hair is really curly too. That might be why it looks short."

Sam and I looked at Lloyd's hair. I have described Lloyd as looking like a young Allen Ginsberg except much hairier. I noticed now that his hair was extremely curly, not just moderately so. It hung from his scalp in ringlets that Shirley Temple would have envied. Each curl was about half an inch wide, and I could easily see how his hair could be twice as long. Lloyd had a tendency to have big hair all the time.

"So, do you like your hair being brown?" I asked.

"Kinda," he said. "I don't like weird colors."

"What about black?" asked Sam.

Lloyd thought about this.

"Sure," said Lloyd. "I'd do that."

"No time like the present," said Sam. "Take a seat."

The razor snapped on again.

"Where'd you learn to read Latin, Lloyd?" I asked.

"I went to Catholic school," he replied. That explained a lot in an instant.

"Yes, but you can read it?" I asked. "That's core."

"I thought it would be cool to be able to converse in a dead language, say things that nobody else would get," he said. "Puns in Latin are truly bad, but it's like puns in Japanese — you can't get them unless you speak the language. I decided I wanted to get to the level of being able to make a pun in Latin. Also, I can rattle off phrases that are funny in modern contexts. Credo Elvum ipsum idiom vivere."

"What does that mean?" Sam and I asked as one.

"I believe that Elvis is still alive," said Lloyd.

"Wow," I said. "So, how did John learn it?"

"I didn't learn it," said John from the doorway. "I found a website called Latin Lingua and got the definitions of each word that way. It also helped me because I could enter partial words and it would figure them out for me."

"Good morning, sorcerer," said Lloyd with heavy sarcasm in his voice.

"Fuck off, Lloyd," said John, moving towards the coffeepot.

"So, how do you know you didn't get anything wrong?" said Lloyd.

"We can check it against the disk you have, can't we?" asked John.

"John," said Sam. "Do you need a haircut?"

I looked at John. His hair was a wreck. He'd last had it braided with extensions, and when the extensions had come out he just hadn't done anything. His hair was still jet black, but it looked kind of sick and hung to his shoulders.

"I need to do something with it," he said.

"Sit down, then," she said.

"Cutting hair?" said Charlie from the door. Yet again, someone had snuck up on us over the buzzing of the clippers.

"Yeah, you need a haircut?" said Sam, hand on her hip.

"My hair is fine," said Charlie. "I have my mother put a bowl on my head and cut it."

"You still live with your mom?" asked Lloyd.

"No, my mom lives with me. There's a difference," said Charlie. "I take care of her."

"Shouldn't you call her?" asked Sam.

"I'll see her when I see her," said Charlie. "She's a tough old bag."

###

We washed the dye out of my hair in the kitchen sink. We had a kitchen sink that someone must have swiped from a restaurant at some point, a large stainless steel tub with single-walled sides. As the last of the purple came out of the sides of my head, I tried not to notice that Sam had one breast pressing against my cheek through her t-shirt as she worked the water through my hair.

"Cathy comes home on Friday," I announced as I sat up. Everyone in the room looked at me, and Sam chose this moment to throw a towel on my head.

"Cool," said John. "Is she still nuts?"

"I think she passed her fit onto the doctor, he's a wreck now," I said.

"I would expect nothing less from Cathy," said Lloyd.

"She's going to love your hair," said Sam, as she handed me a mirror in a frame.

As I examined my new hairstyle, I thought about bringing Cathy back into the fray of our little crusade, if it could be called that.

"We need to tell her about everything that's going on," I said.

"I'm still kind of fuzzy myself," said Sam.

"Yah, why are you people so hip to this magic stuff?" said Charlie. "What made you find me?"

Lloyd and John and I looked at each other, and then it all came tumbling out.

I explained to them how I had met Lloyd, and how Lloyd had told me about the sigil. I told them about the Golden Gate Bridge suicide John and I had seen, and the statues that moved. All three of us recounted the finding the landlord and pressuring him into letting us rent the top part of the house. We told Charlie about the night we were on his bus going to the club when the hopping vampire struck, and then about the nightclub shooting that we really didn't have to explain to anyone.

"And we need Cathy's help," I said. "At the very least, we need her to understand what's going on around her. I need your help to explain all this crap we've been seeing to her."

"Well, you've got my help, but it's probably going to be in that 'I need another chick to help me through this' kind of way," said Sam. "This whole thing is kinda pissing me off."

"I'm along for the ride," said Lloyd.

"Well, yeah," said John.

"I think you're a whacko," said Charlie.

"What?" I asked.

"Grade A nutbag," said Charlie.

"Great," I said. "Then why are you here?"

"You're going to get hurt," said Charlie. "I'm going to try to make sure it's not too bad."

"Great," I said. "Thanks a lot. Real vote of confidence." "Well, you'll understand. At the very least, I've made a bunch of new friends with weird hair," said Charlie.

I had to admit that he was right on that one.

19

The Return

Sam, John, and I piled into John's 1972 Super Beetle to pick Cathy up from the airport. John's car was legendary in our neighborhood. He had turned it into one of the many so-called 'art cars' that seem to be the province of quaint Sunday paper pullouts. John only got interviewed about his car around Halloween.

The entire car had been covered in Astroturf™. He had built a small but sturdy fence that he had hot-glued to the fake grass, and made many tiny headstones out of pieces of plastic that he had carved. He'd built his car out of two junked cars that had been abandoned in his hometown of Seattle, and had modified the pedals so that when he shifted, pressed on the accelerator, or hit the brakes, a different set of zombies popped up from beneath their artificially covered graves. The top of the car had a luggage rack, and all over it there were headstones, as if each different part of the car were a different section of a cemetery. He said he'd modeled it after a cemetery he used to get drunk at in Redmond, that had a set of stairs that led into the earth — the locals said the stairway went to Hell.

John was very noticeable on the road.

The San Francisco airport is located south of the city, across the freeway from South San Francisco. Letters fifty feet high are carved into a hill that is visible from the freeway, proclaiming South San Francisco to be 'The Industrial City'. John always has to make some joke about bands whenever we drive by it.

"Hey look, I hear Front 242 is playing here tonight," he said, downshifting. A miniature Frankenstein monster popped up and laid back down right in front of me as he did so.

"Yes, very funny," I agreed. I held onto the Jesus Bar as the Beetle careened down the freeway and onto the one-hundred-foot-high overpass that led to the airport arrival gates. The Jesus Bar was a steel bar that John had welded on the car's dashboard, where the glove compartment used to be. It had a metal statue of Jesus on either side of it, and it wasn't there for anything more than giving John's passengers comfort in stressful times, such as barreling down Highway 101 at 25 miles an hour over the speed a Beetle should logically travel at.

The San Francisco Airport was undergoing severe construction. An expansion had placed a large building across the road leading into it, a monstrosity of stainless steel and glass that seemed doomed to fall and crush the cars flowing beneath it. There was no damage from the earthquake that we could see at first, but as we approached the structure, we noticed that there was no glass at all in some parts of it. The previous week's shaking must have shattered some of the new glass.

I checked the flight information again and directed John to park in one of the easily identified, color-coded short-term parking lots that led to terminal one. We parked the car in slot number twenty-three of the red lot. John picked the spot out on purpose when he saw the spaces were numbered.

Sam had ended up bleaching her hair and shaving it until there was about a quarter-inch of hair all over her head except for the front. She had braided two long pieces that hung from her temples, and left her bangs hovering somewhere just above her eyebrows. She had taken to wearing cutoff army fatigues and black German Army surplus tank tops with a motorcycle jacket. The rainy season in San Francisco had forced us all to break out the old overcoats — my leather trenchcoat flapped around my ankles and John had on an olive drab Army-issue parka with two-tone patches all over it. We moved through the airport and people moved out of our way.

"Good thing Lloyd isn't here," said John.

"He'd never get past security with that gun," I said.

"Yeah, that's what…" John trailed off as if he remembered something.

"What's up?" Sam asked. She was getting a little bit more gruff in her responses. I carefully considered the line of her jaw and how her cheeks moved when she was chewing gum. It was Sam's body, but her personality was undergoing a marked change. She seemed a bit tougher now.

"I can't get past security," said John.

"You're not packing, are you?" I asked.

John looked nervous.

"Not a gun," he said.

"What is it then?" asked Sam.

"Well," John began. "I have this piercing…" "Stainless steel doesn't set off metal detectors," Sam said.

"Yeah, but…" said John.

"But what?"

"I have a solid iron weight hanging off of it."

"I don't even want to know, John," I said.

"No, you don't," he said.

We stopped at the top of the stairs from the parking and baggage levels. Ahead of us lay the gates, and between here and there was a group of x-ray machines that had a line of people leading away from it towards us. On either side of us lay small shops in which people were sold food, toiletries, and magazines at amazing markups from the normal prices.

"You stay here and wait for us," I said. "It shouldn't take us too long."

Sam and I headed towards the metal detectors.

"You've gone through quite a few changes, Sam," I said.

"No shit," was her reply.

"Well, I hope you don't blame me," I said.

"You didn't cause the earthquake," she said. "You didn't cause that fucknut to go nuts in the nightclub. None of this is your fault."

"I just want it to stop," I said. "I'm trying my best."

"Sooner or later, Derwood," she said, "You're going to have to come to terms with the fact that you can't do jack shit about what's going on."

I thought about it and shut up. She was right — I had no real proof that there actually was a conspiracy to open a gateway to Hell. All the proof of anything was locked up in Lloyd's room being translated from Latin into English so we could all read it and try to interpret it. Lloyd had been cryptic all week, telling us how it was going and that he found some interesting things out today and oh, it'll be done by Friday. It was Friday now, and Lloyd was sleeping in. I hoped he'd have something to show us tonight.

We got to the gate just as the airplane pulled up. We stood silently by a potted palm tree and waited as the jet vomited the passengers into the waiting area. I watched for Cathy among the passengers — she was very easy to spot. I was rather shocked when I saw her, as she had cut her hair in almost the exact style as Sam. I ran to meet her.

"Hey!" she said, putting down a small carry-on bag and meeting me in mid-step. I held her for a while, and then pulled back for a second.

"You cut your hair!" I said.

"So did you!" said Cathy. "And Sam too!"

Sam came up and hugged us too. I found myself considering the shaved heads of my wife and my roommate, and I started to sweat a little bit.

"Come on, John's out at security," I said.

"Why's he there?" asked Cathy, breaking away from me but staying arm in arm with Sam.

"Long story," snickered Sam. "Or at least John wishes it were long."

We walked back up the concourse to the security checkpoint and John.

"I had this really weird dream about you on the plane," said Cathy to John.

"Really?" asked John.

"Yeah, it was you and Sam," she said.

We walked towards the escalators to the baggage area. The escalators were wedged between some glass-fronted exhibits that displayed shoes from around the world.

"We were all at this convention," she began. "It was at some hotel, you know? They all look the same. Anyway, my dear Derwood here wasn't there because it was a pagan convention, and he doesn't believe in things like paganism."

126

"I believe it exists, if you want to quibble over terms," I said.

"Shut up, this is my dream," she said. "At any rate, we were all at this convention, and it was just like that hotel in 'The Shining', you know? It was all ornate and had tons of hallways. The only problem was that all the pagans were really vampires."

"Vampires?" said Sam and John.

"Yeah, vampires, it was weird," said Cathy. "The hotel was full of vampires, and we were running from all the vampires, but they caught us."

"They caught us?" asked John. He seemed to be hanging on her every word.

"Yeah, it was weird," she said. "They bit us all and turned us into vampires too. The thing was that you and me and Sam were the nicest vampires there. All the rest of them were assholes."

"Assholes," said Sam. Sam had fallen into that 'I see this dream is fucked like most of mine are' attitude that usually accompanies a retelling of a dream.

We arrived next to the baggage claim area. The bags were starting to slide down onto the rotating platform for weary travelers to grab.

"Yeah, and we were having a giant vampire ball near the end too. The mean vampires brought a bunch of human beings, and we held them upside down and put little taps in their necks and drank their blood. Then we…" Cathy trailed off.

"What?" asked John. Cathy suddenly blushed.

"Spill it, sister," said Sam.

"Sam and jumped on each other and had lesbian sex on the table," she said, looking embarrassed. "It was really weird, and the whole thing degenerated into an orgy when the vampire-eating flesh demons showed up."

"Vampire-eating flesh demons?" asked John and I.

"You and I did it?" asked Sam. "Wow, cool."

"We were running for our lives, it was weird. I mean, we had supernatural powers and stuff, but these things were huge and they would grab a vampire and just drop them whole into their mouths and chew a few times. They looked kind of like Quentin Tarantino."

"Vampire eating flesh demons that look like giant versions of Quentin

Tarantino," I said.

"Oh, I forgot to tell you, we saw Quentin Tarantino at this Thai restaurant on Melrose," she said.

"Wow, cool," said John. John had worshipped Quentin Tarantino ever since John had worked in that video store.

"Yeah, at any rate, we were running," said Cathy. "And we got to this room with an exit sign. You stopped and said 'We need to make a stand!'"

"Wow," said John.

"Yeah, and Sam and I said 'Fuck that, let's barricade the door and take off, this is the fucking exit!'" said Cathy. "Then I woke up, because the plane was landing."

I spied our dark grey suitcase spilling down the conveyor belt.

"Enlightening," said Sam. She looked at me and winked.

"No, just very fucked up," said Cathy. She grabbed another suitcase and pulled it off, then motioned for me to get the other one.

"What do you think it meant?" I asked.

"It was a dream," said Cathy. "It was my brain taking a dump. It doesn't actually have any significance."

"Derwood finds significance in everything these days," said Sam.

"You say that like it's a bad thing," said Cathy.

"No, it's just understandable and frightening sometimes," said Sam.

Cathy cocked her head. "What do you mean?"

"I think we should continue this discussion in the car," I said.

"Okay," said Cathy. "Lead on."

We moved towards the escalators to the tunnel out to the parking lot. Once we'd strapped ourselves into the colorful Volkswagen, we drove off into the thorny problem of how to explain to Cathy exactly what the hell was going on.

"Let's go to Twin Peaks," I said. "I have to show Cathy something."

We putted towards the city and whatever lay ahead.

20

Twin Peaks

There's a great big honking television tower high on a hill in the middle of San Francisco. It looks like a giant took some kind of three bladed spear-like weapon and threw it straight down onto the hill. In reality it was a device to brainwash millions of people a day with the official stories of the news and entertainment worlds. It'd be a sucky thing to live next to in an earthquake, and evidently it was especially so this time.

The hill in question is called Mount Sutro, after the illustrious ex-Mayor of San Francisco. The television tower is called the Sutro Tower. The Sutro Tower was designed to sway during an earthquake. It was not meant to hold a huge number of additional antennas bolted onto the outside of the structure. According to the newspaper, four of these antennas (weighing in at a good five to ten tons apiece) had broken from their moorings on the Sutro Tower and whipped off down the hillside like arrows from a bow. They had slammed through twenty-six houses and one had ended up impaling a fire station at the base of the hill. The side of the hill looked like a giant scythe had been used to mow down all the houses. Nobody knew the final death toll yet, but the number of missing people lessened each day.

The news kept intoning something about the search for a kid named Davey Wilson, and how not much hope was being held out for finding him safe and sound. Little Davey Wilson's mother and father used to live in a house at the foot of the tower — their house was the first one hit by a giant flying antenna. Mother had regained her senses just long enough to watch as the eight-ton UHF antenna rocketed through the dining room, sharp end first, where father and little Davey Wilson had been crouching under the dining room table, just as the lights went out. She had been spared because it had only torn away half of the house. About a quarter of father had been found already in the remains of the fire station.

Sutro Tower stands on a hill next to two other hills that seem to be identical.There are few antennas on each one, and the ones that are there are very small in comparison. There's a place to park on the top of one, and this was where I was telling John to take us.

We drove up Market Street, past the Café Du Sutro. Cathy stared out the window as we drove past, then she turned around and looked at me.

"I didn't know a single one of those people that died, and yet I felt bad," she said. "Why was that?"

"Because you're human?" I asked.

"Ew, gross," she said.

Sam giggled in the front seat.

"So what do you have to tell me?" she asked, as we crossed Castro Street.

"Well, it's kind of complicated," I said. "I told you before about how the landlord was a serial killer."

Cathy snapped upright.

"What?" she asked.

"I told you before about the landlord," I said.

"You always say weird shit, and usually you only say it once. Why are you talking about this now?" she asked.

"Because the landlord's a serial killer," said Sam and John.

"Oh boy," said Cathy. "Great."

"Well, that's not all," I said. "We've been seeing some really weird things."

"Like the hopping corpse," said Cathy.

"Yeah!" I said. "How'd you remember that?"

"The doctor hypnotized me. I knew what I saw was real. He said I must have fabricated it in my mind, but I know what I saw. He located major incidents of trauma in my recent past, including my new-found fear of buses."

"OK," I said. This was actually a bit better than I expected. Maybe therapy does work after all.

"So there really was a hopping corpse on the bus?" she asked.

"Yes, there was," I said. "But that's only part of what's going on."

"What does the shootout in the club have to do with anything?" asked Cathy.

"That's what I'm saying," said Sam. "Derwood here is convinced that all of this means something."

"It does," I said. "It's connected to the statues."

"Just tell me the whole thing," said Cathy.

"Okay," I began. "When I first met Lloyd, he said something that first caught my ear. He told me that there were ten statues all over San Francisco that formed a pentagram when you connected them with lines. Five statues at the tips of the stars, and five for the inner pentagonal shape."

We came to Twin Peaks Drive, and John hung a sharp right onto it. We zoomed up the street as John shifted and toy zombies popped up to menace us through the glass of the front windshield.

"Well, I went to each of the statues," I continued. "I plotted them out on a map of San Francisco. Lloyd was exactly right — they were within ten feet of where they all needed to be for the pentagram to be exact. This kind of freaked me out a little bit. "

I stared out over the side of the road at the Sutro Tower, and all those ruined houses. I could see helicopters lifting out debris, and men scrambling across the nervous piles of timber that used to be somebody's home.

"I started paying more attention to what was going on around me," I said. "John and I saw a guy commit suicide at the Golden Gate Bridge, and one of the statues turned to look at John. We noticed the landlord. We saw the hopping ghost. I saw a statue turn to look at me in the nightclub when the shootout happened. This is all becoming very strange and I have no idea what is going on. I think it's tied into the pentagram, myself. "

We putted to a stop at the top of the hill. Among the tour buses of elderly Japanese tourists and kids that were coming up to look at the view, we parked the weird little Volkswagen. Pulling ourselves out of the frame, we stood on the edge of the sidewalk to look out over the city. I started pointing.

"There's the Golden Gate. That's where statue number one is. There is Sea Cliff, where the statue of Diana is — that's number two. You can't see number three at all from here, but it's at the Sunset Reservoir out front of it. Number four is over there at the Mission Dolores Park -you'll have to guess which one that is. The last one is out at Fort Mason. Those are the outer limits of the pentagram."

"That's only roughly a pentagram shape," said Sam.

"I figured something out, though," I said. "It was all accounting for the exact length of a line laid over the hills — when the hill was taller, it'd add more length to the side of the pentagram."

"How'd you figure that out?" ask John.

"I lay awake one night thinking about it," I said. "It just occurred to me that it must have been the way they did it, and I tried walking one entire side. It was kind of hard to do, but it roughly corresponded with what size the line should have been. The two points at the top are in roughly the same elevation — it's the other three that were walked out this way."

"We have one of these statues for the inner pentagon near our house — it's in the Panhandle Park. We don't know much about them, but I am going to go to the library tomorrow and look up what I can about each of those statues."

"I wanna help," said Sam.

"I'll go with you," said Cathy.

"You don't think this is nuts?" I asked.

"It's interesting," said Cathy. "Insanity is very, very interesting,"

"Is that a reference to me, or are you commenting on your mental state?" I asked.

"Both," she said.

###

I didn't talk the rest of the way home. I was in very deep thought. Cathy and Sam were in the back seat talking about something in low tones. John just drove and seemed happy with the attention that his car got. We walked up the stairs after extricating Cathy's luggage from the rooftop rack, and struggled under the weight of it. Sam and Cathy kept chattering as Lloyd opened the door on us. They walked right on up the stairs and into Sam's room.

"I figured a lot of stuff out, man," he said.

"Do tell," I said as I moved into the foyer and deposited the bags net to the door.

"Well, I have all the writing deciphered and it's exactly what I thought it was — it's someone's spell book," he began as we walked into the living room. "He left a lot of notes for this big ritual that he did."

"Why was he involved?" I asked.

"Because he lived close to the statue that he did rituals over," said Lloyd. "Evidently, this all had to happen consecutively for three hundred days — the desecration of the statue to TUTIVILLUS."

"Say what?" asked John.

"A minor demon," said Lloyd. "Demons all have purposes. Some of the older ones are lord of the flies or lord of the itchy bowels, or whatever. TUTIVILLUS was the demon that collected all the words and fragments of words that are misspoken or missaid by priests in sermons and brings them all back to Hell to stoke the fires. A demon of nit-picking, if you will."

"A demon of nit-picking?" asked John. "That sounds like an ex-girlfriend of mine."

"Funny, ha ha," said Lloyd. "Look, I can't help you do this."

"Why not?" I asked.

"Because when I signed up for the Hell holiday package," said Lloyd, "I most specifically did not want the part of hell where they nitpick you to death for all eternity. No way am I crossing this guy. That's the only parts of this that you can affect — we don't know what the other statues have been desecrated to. It will only take three nights of rituals to undo the three hundred nights, though."

"Well, thanks for the tips, Lloyd," I said.

"Hey, nothing personal," said Lloyd. "You know how it is, as I'm supposed to follow these guys."

"Yeah, but you're one of the ones that's going to die," I said. "Don't you think you'd better practice what you preach and only look out for yourself?"

Lloyd looked like he actually considered this for a moment, and then that moment lasted a little bit longer and the entire idea blossomed in his head.

"Hey, yeah," he said. "I'm supposed to be a selfish follower of Satan. I'm going to run away now."

"I bet you that if we don't do something, things are going to get even more fucked up," I said. "I bet that demon will be released."

"You might be right," said Lloyd. "But I am telling you — I don't want to be anywhere near this shit."

"Just shut up and tell me what we have to do, Lloyd," I said. "I'm too tired to deal with your bullshit."

###

I finished arguing with Lloyd and stomped upstairs to our bedroom with the luggage. I managed to get the door open and dropped the bags at the foot of our bed. Cathy and Sam were sitting on the bed as I came in, and turned to look at me as I trudged over to the bed and took my shoes off.

"You and Lloyd kiss and make up?" asked Cathy.

"No, he finally heard what I was saying," I said. I lay down on my side of the bed.

"What were you saying?" asked Sam.

"That he'd better not back down after he promised me he'd help me," I said.

"Lloyd's a weasel," said Cathy. "Don't trust him."

"Yeah, he'll screw you over," said Sam. I might have heard this, but I can't say for certain because I fell asleep. The only reason I do is because I was told what happened after I went to sleep.

134

21

Rude Awakening

I awoke to the smell of coffee as sunlight poured into our room. My arm was asleep, and I was in that fuzzy, half-awake state that most people are in when they first sit up in the morning. I wasn't sitting — I was still lying down. I struggled to push myself up and then I noticed that the bed was rather crowded, even though the bed was king-sized.

Cathy and Sam had evidently just crawled into bed and talked all night. Cathy was the reason my arm was asleep, and Sam was on the other side of Cathy. I moved careful to avoid waking anyone up, but I was unsuccessful.

"Good morning," Sam whispered over Cathy.

"Good morning," I whispered back. "What are you doing in my bed?"

"I didn't feel like sleeping alone last night," whispered Sam.

"Huh?" said Cathy, groggily.

"Great," I whispered. I had just discovered that in a bed with three people in it, everyone usually wakes up at the same time.

"You're not mad at me, are you?" whispered Sam.

"You can stop whispering, I'm awake now," said Cathy."And he's not mad, he's just grumpy when he wakes up."

"Just kind of startled," I replied. "It's not every day that I get two women with the same hairstyle in the same bed."

"Yeah, the question now is whether or not you'll know what to do," said Sam, wryly.

I eyed Sam suspiciously. Cathy giggled.

"Really, my love," said Cathy. "Isn't it every guy's dream to get two women in bed?"

I started eyeing Cathy suspiciously at this point, and she giggled again.

"I think we'll have to show him," said Sam.

"Yes, I think we will," giggled Cathy, She grabbed Sam, rolled her on top of her, and kissed her.

"Nice joke," I said. "You almost had me going for a second."

I got up and left them giggling in the bed.

###

I descended the stairs following the scent of coffee. John was sitting at the table with Charlie.

Charlie had gone back to his house in Chinatown to find it a complete wreck. It took him a week to clean it up, and he had stayed with some friends in Chinatown. He visited a lot more often, and didn't seem put off by John rolling joints at breakfast.

"Hey, how's it going?" asked Charlie.

"Good seeing you again, Charles," I said soberly. "It appears to be a lot better this morning that I expected it to be."

"That's always a good one," said Charlie. "I'm just telling John here about my bad news."

"What bad news?" I asked.

"My apartment building got condemned," said Charlie. "Nowhere to stay now."

"What about your mother?" asked John.

"She's tough," said Charlie. " She also has some money saved up. She is going to take a trip back to China and stay with some of our family for a while."

"Well, what are you going to do?" I asked.

"I dunno," said Charlie. "Rent is dropping really fast, so I may just start looking for a new apartment."

In 1989, the Loma Prieta earthquake did absolutely nothing for the rental market in San Francisco. Prices went up, if anything. This earthquake was considerably stronger than the one in 1989 — the seismologists agreed that this earthquake was an eight on the Richter scale. The Richter scale is kind of hard to understand until you realize that every time you go up one number, it's ten times stronger than the last number on the scale. The quake was about that much stronger than the one in 1989. The city was trashed, even though power had been restored overnight.

"We'll have to have a house meeting about it, but I think you can stay here until you find a place of your own," I said.

"I already told him that," said John. He licked the joint and stuck it behind his ear, which made me resolve not to take a puff off this one.

"I have my stuff in the car," he said. "Is that room I slept in the other night still free?"

"Yup," I said. "Don't get too comfortable."

"Why's that?" he asked.

"The landlord's a serial killer," said Lloyd as he moved into the kitchen. "And he lives in the basement."

"Great," said Charlie. "Just what I need."

We watched Charlie walk out the front door, and I turned back to face Lloyd.

"Anything new?" I asked.

"Yeah, I think," said Lloyd. "But I don't believe it myself."

"Okay," I said. "It must be pretty weird for you to say that."

"It's not a gateway," said Lloyd.

"Really?" asked John. "Then what is it?"

"I think it's a force field," said Lloyd.

"What makes you say that?" I asked.

"It's a giant protection sigil," said Lloyd.

"But what would it protect against?" I asked.

"Hell if I know," said Lloyd. "But there most definitely is not a gateway to Hell being opened up here."

The entrance of Cathy ended the speculation. She glided through the door in one of my tweed bathrobes, and grabbed two mugs from a dryer rack.

"Hey love," she said. "I'll be upstairs."

"I'm just chatting with Lloyd," I said. "He's talking about the book the landlord gave us."

"That's pleasant, dear," said Cathy as she gathered the cups up in her hands and moved out the door. "Come back up when you get a chance."

"I'll tell you later," said Lloyd.

Charlie walked in at the same time I was moving to go out.

"Thank you, guys," said Charlie. "I thank your wife too, she was on the stairs."

"Oh great," said John.

"Great indeed," I said. "She's going to go tell Sam and this is before we all consulted with them."

"Shit!" said Lloyd, and we all turned around to see Cathy and Sam standing in the doorway with angry looks on their faces.

"Okay," said Sam. "Who said this man could move in here?"

"We were coming to talk to you two," said John.

"I walked in on them plotting it," said Lloyd.

"I'm completely to blame, blame me," I said.

"Shut up, Jesus," said Cathy. "We're not done yet."

###

It turned out to be much worse than we expected. After hearing Charlie's story, Cathy and Sam made us let Charlie's mother stay with us until they made other arrangements. We watched as Charlie guided his mother up the stairs — the woman seemed ancient, with a face like soft creased leather and the stature of a dwarf. Charlie had mentioned that she was in her 60's, but she was peculiarly alien as she didn't speak very much English. Her hair was snow white, and was braided in a single tail down the middle of her back.

"Mother requests that you not smoke so much reefer around her," said Charlie. "It makes her feel funny."

"No problem," said Lloyd.

The woman set about in her room unpacking a couple of large trunks that she made Charlie carry up the stairs.

She stood on the landing and said something incoherent.

"Mother wonders if you would mind if she cooked up some of her medicine?" asked Charlie.

"Sure, go ahead," said John. "Unless the smell will make us feel funny."

"Maybe not then," said Charlie.

"Whoa, wait a minute, she can go ahead," said Lloyd. "I'm all into feeling funny."

The ancient woman walked down the stairs with a small case and a strangely shaped pot. The pot was entirely made of clay, and had a spout protruding from the front of it. A cylinder protruded from the body at a point that was ninety degrees from the spout and offset forty-five degrees from the plane of the surface the pot would sit upon. A small clay lid was secured on the top. She walked towards the kitchen, and Lloyd followed her.

"I need to go practice," said Charlie.

I decided to watch for myself. I padded after Charlie, and followed him through the kitchen where his mother was gabbering in Chinese at Lloyd.

"Right on, grandma," said Lloyd. "I have some stuff that's like medicine in my room if you want some of that too."

She looked at him, and said what were probably some of the only words she knew in English.

"Smart ass."

I chuckled as I walked through the old screen door and onto the porch. I watched from the wooden railing as Charlie walked out to the center of the grass. He bent over and laid his palms on the undersides of his feet, stretching his muscles. John stepped up to the railing beside me as Charlie melted into a series of flowing circles with his limbs. He held his back very straight and moved very slowly. His feet were pointed slightly outwards, and his knees were bent at a shallow angle.

"Tai Chi," said John.

"No shit," I said.

"I had an idea today," said John.

"What's that?" I asked.

"Well, this big pentacle will only work if it's completely intact, right?" he asked.

"Yes, but it's nothing threatening at all," I said. "You heard Lloyd, it's just some kind of a Satanic blessing."

"Yeah, but who knows?" he asked. "Maybe that's a good thing to have, a bit of protection."

"From what?" I asked. "There's nothing to protect against."

"How do you know?" he asked.

"I'm not prepared to debate the existence or non-existence of God," I said. "I really wish I'd never started on this whole pentagram kick."

"Yeah, but a pentagram of protection will only work if it's completely intact," he said. "And out here in California, the ground tends to move."

I suddenly saw his point. For some reason, I became nervous. Out of the corner of my eye, Charlie flowed a little faster.

Cathy broke the silence by coming onto the back porch.

"Hey honey, we got invited to a party," she said.

I looked at John, and then back at Cathy.

"Oh yeah?" I asked. "Who is it?"

"It's Annabel and Julian," she said. "It's dinner at the Cliff House."

"Tell them we're coming," I said as Cathy faded back into the house.

"Okay," she called back at me as she retreated.

"We've got a party to go to," I said. Charlie was moving faster than any Tai Chi I'd ever seen, but with the same fluid movements. John was staring at him, and I was too.

"Why?" asked John, not taking his eyes off Charlie.

"Because then we'll have an excuse to check on Diana," I said.

"Okay," said John.

In the garden below us, Charlie planted his feet, extended his arms, and made a slight shrug. His arms raised slightly, and we heard a loud crack as the fabric of his shirt slapped against his shoulders and burst at the seams. The shirt puffed out a bit, and then fell around him, ragged and torn.

"I ruined an old shirt to show you my trick," he said. "I have to be careful, shirts are expensive."

The stench of exotic medicines made us lightheaded, and we walked back inside to plot our next move.

22

The Cliff House

The Cliff House stands on a lonely crag that overlooks the Pacific Ocean, jutting into the sea further than any other point in San Francisco. Today it isn't even a shadow of its former self — it's a drab block of building that sits on the foundation of the former restaurant. There's a penny arcade in the basement made up of machines from an amusement park called Funland that used to sit less than a quarter mile from the building.

The first Cliff House was a small blocky building built on the sea. The first one was rather boring.

The second Cliff House was a huge Victorian mansion that perched precariously between a cliff and the sea. Spires rose against the blue-grey background and the wide rolling view of the waves made it a favorite of San Francisco. It was still a 'swank' restaurant, if cinderblock and overpriced food made up your definition of 'swank'. It was still the nicest dining view in San Francisco.

"It's fucking cold," said Lloyd. We piled out of a large minivan painted in the colors of the Veteran's Taxicab Company of San Francisco to the waiting party.

"Crowds suck," said Cathy, pulling her faux leopard coat around her.

The current Cliff House stood before us. It was once again a boring, blocky building by the sea. I surveyed it and grimly stuck to my thought that this would be where we spent the last night of the year – when Cathy announced the party invitation, I hadn't actually registered the fact that it was on New Year's Eve.We hadn't even thought about going to a party on New Year's Eve yet – we all had other things on our minds. It suddenly snapped into place for me that we should go to this party, and we sent an RSVP asking if our roommates could come.

Julian and Annabel were an interesting pair. Julian was another one of the stock market dot com paper millionaires that seemed to infest the city these days like termites. His wealth enabled him to provide Annabel, his 'primary' relationship, with a lot of money for shopping. Their posturing fooled nobody. Julian was pretty much whipped into submission by Annabel, who had that poor boy convinced he could do anything he wanted with anyone he wanted. This is one of the reasons I usually cite when I tell people I like women more than I do men – they can perform incredible feats of dominance while smiling nicely.

None of this hid the fact that they were a pathetically strange couple. Obsessed with money, they rented out the Cliff House to host a party for the crowd that Julian kept – Swedish businessmen, New York media mavens, and strange webzine editors. We fit among none of those, but Catherine had once worked at a sex store in SOMA and had sold Annabel many interesting outfits that involved saddles and butt plugs made out of horsehair. This garnered her an invitation to Annabel's party and her 'friends' were to be brought along as a bit of local color. I grimly reflected on how the poor old Cliff House was a tourist trap to its last gasping breath. I went out of fondness for something I had never known but had seen majestic pictures of, and I thought it might be nice to wander among the rich outlanders on the former grounds of 1920's decadence. We'd been to their parties before, and I decided not to tell Lloyd and John what to expect.

"Hello, sweeties!" squealed Annabel. This was the bit I didn't like about Annabel – she squealed a bit much until she got calm over seeing you again. Annabel was forty years old, blonde, had on a black patent leather corset and not much else.

"Hello there!" said Cathy brightly. I usually let Cathy handle these

143

conversations, as I really didn't know what to say to a woman I knew had bought a saddle to ride her common law husband around like a pony with.

"Who are your friends?" asked Annabel. She squealed less this time – she must have been getting drunk already. Julian walked up wearing a gimp mask.

Cathy pulled Sam up to the front and hugged her.

"This is Sam, and that's Lloyd," she said, " and that over there is John and Charlie is in the back there."

"How do you do?" asked Charlie with a slight bow.

"Pleasure to meet you," said John with a slight bow.

"Yo, Annie, what's up?" asked Lloyd. Lloyd had been snorting little spoonfuls of a white powder in celebration of the New Year, and we'd complained about it in the car when he'd sneezed and gotten it everywhere. It was extremely unhip to be snorting white powders in the City these days, and I suspected Lloyd of wanting to start trouble to ring in the New Year. I vowed to keep an eye on him myself before we left the house.

"How'd the year go by so fast?" squealed Annabel. "The last year of the millennium!"

"That's next year," three of us said at once. I looked around at Sam and John and saw it on Lloyd's lips. Annabel looked like a robot that had had a button pushed.

"Silly me!" she said. "Why next year?"

"Because the first year didn't start at zero", I said. "It started at one A.D. Besides, it's a screwed up calendar anyway."

"Yeah, where's the booze?" asked Lloyd.

"Right this way," smiled Annabel, who sensed a graceful exit to the conversation.

\###

The crowd was uglier than we had expected.A lot of the people were talking about the terrible tragedy on the night of the earthquake. Things had rattled everyone in the city, and the only people who came out for comfort on New

Years Eve were the most desperate of people, those who had nowhere else to go and had decided at the last minute that they should at least do something. Being Julian's friends, they were all dripping with money. The problem with money is that it truly doesn't buy anything, and on New Year's Eve a lot of accidentally rich people were sitting around with their thumbs up their asses trying to figure out what to do.

I had suspected it might be this way, but I had no idea of how truly bad it would be. We couldn't bear the party for more than thirty minutes. I talked to a marketing rep, the CEO of a software startup, three programmers, and a woman whose husband had died of a heart attack after guiding his search engine website through an initial public offering. Of the six, the woman was the most interesting – she was only twenty-nine.

"I married my husband for his money," she said. "I just had no idea he'd kick off so soon!"

"Nice," I said.

"Well, I have to laugh somehow," she said. "Otherwise I'd be crying, right?"

"Um, right," I said.

I looked her up and down. She was wearing black. I decided it was a widow thing.

"I have to go," I said. "My wife needs saving from that Swedish business-man."

I moved away and into the path of an enraged Lloyd Stark. He looked enraged, at least.

"I'm having fun, man!" he said. "Give me another person with funny-colored hair to hit!"

"Can we leave, Lloyd?" I asked.

"I thought you would never ask me," said Lloyd with a grin. "I'm only kidding about the funny-colored hair."

We gathered Sam, and John, and Charlie. We bid our goodbyes to the hosts, begging other parties where we were needed. This was the one excuse that we knew would get us out of a party anywhere, because everyone was party-hopping. This was one of the rules of party-going – the more parties you had to go to, the more popular you were. We were adept at figuring out ways to use these boneheaded social rules to our own twisted advantage. Tonight, the party had given us an excuse to check on Diana the Hunter.

Diana was a statue that sat on the grounds of the Sutro Estate overlooking the Cliff House. This was publicly accessible because Sutro had opened his estate to the public and by city tradition it had remained a city park ever since. We had to walk up a large hill from the Cliff House to the park gates, and we wheezed as we struggled past parking lots and bus stops for a long city block away from the sea.

In the space of this city block, the land rises nearly one hundred feet. The estate once existed on a cliff that overlooked the Cliff House itself, and we wandered around the estate drinking from a bottle of whiskey that Lloyd had smuggled out of the party.

"Jack Black," said Lloyd, and he drank a pull from the bottle.

"Give me that," said Sam as she grabbed the bottle away from Lloyd.

We wandered over to the area that the statue resided in.

"This was the last statue installed," said Lloyd. "These guys didn't use any particular imagery for the statues."

"Crazy," said Charlie.

The area was a footpath about ten feet wide. Lloyd pulled a heavy flashlight from the folds of his trenchcoat, and I started to suspect him of keeping a utility belt underneath his coat. The beam illuminated foliage on either side of the path, and then fell upon the statue.

The woods here were punctuated by the sound of the ocean in the distance. Trees loomed menacingly as we pushed branches away from our eyes. We moved towards the clearing and finally gazed upon her form with no annoying undergrowth to block our view. Diana had wreaths of flowers at her feet, left there by neo-pagans who thought they understood their own offerings.

"Hey, cool," said Sam, and then she abruptly disappeared from the light while cursing.

"What the fuck?" asked Sam.

"You OK?" asked John. Cathy moved towards where we had seen Sam last, as Lloyd played the beam over where Sam had fallen.

Sam had tripped over a long gash in the ground, going on as far as we could see. It wasn't very deep, but the earth had sunk about four inches on one side of the crack. As Lloyd shone his flashlight over it, I had my old sense of weirdness flood over me. The gash was obviously induced by the earthquake – it was the entire cliff the estate was on, slipping a little bit into the sea. We saw the grim news as Lloyd followed the crack in the earth.

"Shit," said Lloyd. "The statue is on the seaward side of this crack."

"Let's see what is up," I said, and I pulled out another gadget that I kept beside my police scanner. I had made a wise investment in a GPS receiver, and I hoped that the satellites wouldn't all fail at midnight and render it useless.

The device had a crude memory in it – you could record up to twelve locations in it. We were currently at location number ten from my initial survey, and I set the device on the base of the statue.

The little device read out — Lat: 37.778479 Lon: -122.510031.

Maps are based on longitude and latitude. Most people never have to use these things in real life, but I had to summon all of my memories of high school to tell me how badly we were screwed by the fissure in the ground. A degree of longitude was sixty nautical miles. The device read out that the latitude of the current location was 37.778480 and the longitude was –122.51004. This meant that the statue had moved by about 30 feet, give or take a few inches. Not good.

"Well, this thing is only accurate to within a few meters," I said. "It could be wrong."

"It's moved, hasn't it?" asked Cathy.

"It looks that way," I admitted.

"We're all getting worked up over nothing," said John. "I mean, before this Lloyd was babbling about it being a protection."

Lloyd started to speak. When Lloyd gets frustrated, he sometimes looks upward as if to dare someone to prove him wrong. This time, that might have happened. He kept looking, and we all looked upward to see what he was looking at.

In the sky, a small white dot was getting brighter and moving.

"What is that?" asked Sam.

"It's almost midnight," I said. "I bet it's some kind of fireworks. Let's run up to the ruins of the mansion and get a better look."

We all looked at each other for a second, and I realized that maybe we should do that no matter what it was.

We had made it about 200 feet when we heard a low rumble. As we ran to the foundation, I looked upward. The object had grown considerably in brightness but not noticeably in size. It glowed a bright white and the only thing I could think of was a missile or a bomb.

We reached the foundation of the house in time to see the final seconds of the fireball's flight. It had passed over our heads and was heading out to sea. I held Cathy as we watched the fireball descend upon the Farralon Islands, lighting them up with a flash. A few moments of grotesque silence followed, as Lloyd said, "I sure hope that wasn't anything nuclear..."

I looked down at the Cliff House with Annabel and Julian's party still writhing onward in it. As I watched, I saw the water in the coastline recede ever so slightly. The white waves were barely visible through the fog, but I thought I saw the mast of a ship tilting at a crazy haphazard angle among them as I thought about starting to move backwards, and then the big wave hit.

Sea foam and salt spray shot straight up in front of our faces into the fog, and a few tons of water fell down upon the sturdy concrete brick of the Cliff House. I suddenly realized that I couldn't hear anything for the wind and the loud cracking boom that accompanied it, but we all ran backwards away from the edge of the cliff with our ears ringing and our knees shaking.

"Can you hear me?" yelled Cathy.We all were bent over in the howling wind, and one by one we checked each other. The wind showed no sign of abating, yet Lloyd walked back over to the edge of the cliff and peered downward.

"Fuck!" screamed Lloyd.

"What is it?" we yelled, and then we were running to the edge.

As we peered down at the people spilling out of the Cliff House, Lloyd cursed his luck and screamed at the heavens.

"What kind of a moronic god fashions apocalyptic disasters and fails to take out all the rich perverts during the end times?" he screamed. "Why even bother if you can't do one simple thing?"

God pissed down his answer in Lloyd's face.

23

Songs You'll Never See In the Same Light Again

"They're saying it was a meteor or a comet!" said John, excitedly. Sunday morning breakfast was more lively this millennium, as we had an amazing new natural disaster to watch unfold on the television. Downstairs, our landlord was playing "Maneater" by Hall and Oates at full volume. I didn't want to think of what he was actually doing in time to the music.

Breakfast brought upsetting images of smashed sea lions on the Farralons and great white sharks feeding off the carcasses being pushed into the water spilled across the tube. A large smoking crater had been found on a long rocky beach, and it had pummeled one of the islands into shattering like glass, spraying a large sea lion breeding ground with flying hunks of supersonic granite. The shock wave had raised a wave about fifty feet high, and when it got to Ocean Beach it had smashed against the seawall and killed a few dozen hippies camping on the beach. The Sutro Baths had been almost totally obliterated, the sandy hillside melting into the sea under the force of tons of water. The zoo had been flooded, and somehow a monkey had been left stranded atop the old Doggie Diner sign, sitting on the doggie chef 's nose.

Lloyd moved to the blackboard and wrote 'Maneater, Hall and Oates' at the bottom of a long list of songs and artists.

The blackboard in the kitchen had once been installed as a way of communication for the house. It had turned into a list of Songs that You Would Never See In The Same Light Again. This was basically a list of songs that our serial killing landlord had blared at one time or another at top volume to cover the sound of his heavy electric power tools. It was a litany of 70's and 80's music.

Blondie, Heart of Glass was on the list. So was Duran Duran's 'Hungry like the Wolf'. Sam had jokingly given him an Einstürzende Neubauten CD on the premise that his tools would blend right in to the music, and he'd returned it the next day, saying it was too suspicious-sounding and made him very nervous for some reason. The next weekend, we had gone right back to the 80's with the Missing Persons and Dead or Alive.

I tried not to think about why he was playing the music, but it was a little hard not to think about. The strange thumps sometimes suggested that he'd gotten a live one downstairs and was merrily bashing in their skull in the name of his psoriasis to the tune of ' It's My Life' by Talk Talk. Other times I listened in horror as my favorite Thomas Dolby songs were accompanied by an annoying high-pitched buzzsaw whine that altered as if it had entered some sort of solid tissue. He never borrowed music from us again – he claimed our music was too disturbing and dark, and shunned our offerings of Ministry and Nine Inch Nails in favor of something nice and happy by Abba. You've never had a restless night from imagining someone deboning a human body while blaring 'Waterloo' or 'Fernando'. It's not fun.

"The TV said that it was probably about fifty to seventy five feet across, and came shooting in so fast that it was probably a lot larger but boiled away in the atmosphere. We saw it! How cool!"

"John," I said, "That could just as easily been a bit bigger and we wouldn't be here. In fact, it could have easily been bigger than that and killed off this hemisphere."

"Fact is, Derwood, it didn't," said Lloyd. He paused as the music changed, and after a second of thinking, he wrote down 'Super Freak, Rick James'.

"It's a little weird, isn't it, Lloyd?"

"Life is weird," said Lloyd. He had a point.

"It still all makes me very nervous," I said.

"Of course it does," said Cathy as she walked into the kitchen. My girlfriend was dressed in an old silk kimono I had bought for her in New Orleans, and she walked over to the coffeepot intent on draining a cup of it.

"What?" I said.

"You've got an amazing imagination," she said. "You've probably got it all interconnected in your head somehow with those statues."

"No, I don't!" I said angrily. "Look, you might think I'm crazy, but even I can't connect the dots between a big rock falling from the sky and a bunch of old loony pagans trying to redefine the map of San Francisco."

"Well, you might not be far off with that," said Lloyd. "A spell might have been cast against things like that rock falling out of the sky."

"Explain," I said.

"Well, you know in that part in the Bible?" asked Lloyd. "The one where all those people die?"

I snickered.

"You mean the flood?" asked John.

"He means Old Testament in general," said Cathy. "Fire and brimstone hogwash. Things to keep the masses in fear of God."

"Yeah," said Lloyd. "So what if our Satanists believe in that Yahweh and decide to cast a spell so that Yahweh can't smite the city and turn anyone who looks back into a pillar of salt?"

"That's the best explanation I've heard all day," said John.

"We got invited to another party," said Cathy. She moved towards the door without another word.

###

There's an interesting truism about parties in San Francisco. There will be long periods of time with horrible parties, and then a few really cool and neat parties all clustered together in the same period of time. The trick when party-hopping is to try and hit the good ones. This means you get some bad ones. You just have to keep trying and hibernate for a while when things start going bad.

It had been almost a year since the party incident involving Cathy's ruined birthday, and we had mostly been paying attention to our own affairs since then. Lloyd made the rounds of the party circuit and assured us for the better part of a year that all of the parties around were truly lame. Our weird New Year's Eve plans had whetted our appetites for some parties with people we could relate to, and we decided to put our feelers out for better fare. Lloyd had promptly suggested crashing several important Masonic functions he knew of.

Sam ended up getting us house invitations to other house parties. San Francisco communal households sometimes make up quaint bonding names like "House of Deviant Normalcy" or "Chateau Marmoset". We'd never made up a name for our odd collection of roommates, but we felt we didn't need to most of the time. We knew we were different from them. Protocol eventually dictated that we make something up.

"I told them we were 'Pee Wee Dahmer's Playhouse'," said Sam when she addressed the Sunday Breakfast.

"Not bad," said Lloyd. "I personally would have just kept to the Family theme Manson loved so much."

"Cut it out, you fiends," I said. "Sam, tell us about these people."

"Well," she said. "They're a bunch of art school musicians. Really snooty."

"Perfect," I said. "We're instantly cooler than them."

"They're popular with the club kids," she continued. "Mostly because they have lots of free alcohol at their parties."

"Hey, I'm down," said Lloyd.

"They love drama," she said. "They often invite people they know will cause trouble."

"We are so there," said Lloyd. Sam looked at him wryly.

"Can we all go?" asked Charlie. "Ma doesn't like parties, but I do. The last one was boring. Maybe I can break up a fight at this one."

"You know what happens when you hit a goth?" I asked Charlie. He shook his head.

"They cry," we said in chorus at Charlie.

"Where is it?" I asked.

"It's in the Mission," said Sam.

"We'll go," I said, mentally reminding myself to walk near the statue in Mission Dolores Park.

Lloyd used the chalk to write in "Billy Idol, Eyes Without a Face."

24

How to Succeed at Suicide

We walked about fifteen blocks from our place in the Haight to the party in the Mission. Walking is the preferred mode of transportation in San Francisco, because the buses suck and parking is really a bitch. When you find a parking spot, it's a wise idea to camp out on it for a while — at least until they're about to ticket you for being parked there on street cleaning day.

"Whose party is this again?" asked John. He carried a hefty backpack.

"It's this kid we know," said Cathy. "His name is Seth. It's him and his roommates."

To say that Seth was suicidal was an understatement. I had known Seth for five years, and during that time he had unsuccessfully tried to commit suicide about twelve times. He was legendary in the San Francisco scene for his parties, which usually climaxed with him trying some form of suicide at the end of the night and being taken away.

He was a lanky fellow, with a perpetually down-turned mouth. He usually wore some band t-shirt with a black fabric vest over it, and black jeans to fit his spindly legs. He had crucifix-shaped scars on his wrists -across for the hospital, down for the morgue. Of course, it was always for the hospital with Seth.

Seth lived on Capp Street in the Mission. It's one of the most colorful neighborhoods in the city. Nobody there looks like they are up to any good. We probably didn't look that nice ourselves as we cruised into the neighborhood.

Lloyd took up the front of our flying wedge. He was dressed in a top hat with a snake skeleton and woodpecker skull on it. His leather trench-coat billowed out behind him like wings.

John and Charlie followed him up. John never really dressed up to go to parties. His usual attire of black PVC pants and a t-shirt was good for any occasion. Charlie was a different matter.

"I want to get dressed up," Charlie had said. "I want to look cool."

Charlie was wearing a pair of standard black Chinese slippers with a dark beige sole. As an added bonus, Cathy had lent him one of her skirts. A velvet Nehru jacket from Sam completed the ensemble, and then had come the makeup.

Charlie was shocked at how good he thought he looked, but he was even more perplexed by the fact that nobody stared at him as we walked through the Mission.

"I was sure I'd have been laughed at by now," he said.

"It's the way you carry yourself, Charlie," I said. "You look like you're ready to beat the shit out of everyone."

Following up Charlie and John were Cathy, Sam, and myself in the middle. I had started wearing wool slacks and turtlenecks. Cathy favored leopard print jackets and black shapeless dresses to hide her pregnancy. Sam was wearing a black slip and a long black vintage coat trimmed with monkey fur.

John had the backpack with the GPS receiver in it. While we were at this party, we were going to take a side trip to the statue nearest to the party and measure its position relative to the measurements I had first taken. The statue of Diana was off by more than thirty feet from where it had been before, and we were starting to be fearful of the weird things that would happen when we discovered how far off the other statues were — but we had to check.

Sam wasn't smiling. I hadn't seen her smile since Barnabas had died. Cathy, on the other hand, seemed very happy. Since she had come back from Los Angeles, she and Sam had gotten even closer as friends. I had noticed this and encouraged it, as I had very little time outside of work to pay attention to her. It seemed to be good for Sam too, but I noticed that Sam had started spending more time running her website than associating with real human beings. Working the door at the nightclubs wasn't like dealing with real human beings to Sam, and I understood that.

The party we were going to would, hopefully, be populated with real human beings. In reality, this never holds up. Everyone wears their best mask at a party, and among all of us only Charlie thought it was going to be any fun or interesting.

"We never get to talk, Derwood my love," whispered Cathy in my ear.

"I know," I said. We had avoided talking about the pregnancy in front of other people, and it seemed that we had not had a free moment since Cathy had gotten home to talk about it.

"Well?" she asked.

"Well what?" I asked back.

"What do you want to do?" she asked.

We slowed, letting the others walk ahead of us. Sam noticed, as she was right next to us, and sped up to walk next to Charlie.

"What do you mean, what do I want to do?" I asked.

"Do you want to keep it?" she asked.

"Well, duh," I said. "Haven't you been listening to me?"

"Listening? I'm sorry, you must have said something I didn't catch."

"A long time ago I told you my views about marriage, correct?"

"Yes, it was something about…"

"Marriage should only be instituted in order to take care of children in a relationship," I said. "So let's get married."

"Wow, I didn't know you had it memorized so rigidly," she smirked.

"Well, it applies here," I said.

"Why?" Cathy asked.

"Because if I didn't want a kid, I wouldn't want to marry you," I said.

"Oh," she said, dejected.

"Why the long face?" I asked.

"I dunno," she said. "You wouldn't marry me if you just loved me?"

"Do you not want to have a kid?" I asked.

"Not really," she said. "The more I think about it, the more it depresses me."

"Well, ultimately, it's up to you," I said. "I'll support whatever decision you make."

"Well, it's not really our decision anymore," said Cathy.

"What?" I asked.

"I've been carrying it too long to terminate it. No reason really to terminate it."

"So, we're going to have it?" I asked.

I watched her face as she sucked in a breath and held it.

"Yup," she said.

"I guess you'd better learn to live with it," I said. "Do you want to get married?"

"Forget that," she said. "What are we going to tell the roommates?"

###

"Hello, guys," said Seth as he opened the door. "You're about the only cool people here."

Seth's place was a flat in the Mission close to the park and one of the last cemeteries inside San Francisco. He shared it with a group of kids from the local art college. We walked into a foyer that was already filled with people. Seth was being depressed as usual, and moaning that nobody showed up to the party. He began to get irritating. We lost him in the kitchen, where John and Lloyd caught the scent of alcohol and food.

The norm around San Francisco applied here — about ten kids lived in a four-bedroom flat. The only difference was that they had some very unusual rules for membership in their household. Cathy and I hadn't let anyone in on this little fact.

"These people creep me out," said Sam.

"Don't say it too loud," hissed Cathy.

"What's wrong here?" asked Sam.

"Let's go out and get a smoke on the deck," said Cathy.

"OK," said Sam.

"We'll stay here," I said.

"You do that," said Cathy.

The kitchen was a sordid affair. Most slumlords in San Francisco hadn't done any work on the kitchens in nearly thirty years, and this flat was no different. An ancient, grease-covered stove held several pizza boxes in various stages of disarray. The laminate counters from the sixties held every manner of liquor. The sink was full of ice and beer. Looking around at the ceilings, you could see the accumulation of one cooking accident after another. The place was a mess, yet had been cleaned as best it could be for this party.

As I wondered why my girlfriend was getting punchy, I looked over at a girl who was standing by the refrigerator. She was eyeing John.

As girls go, she was homely. She had large, thick glasses with plastic frames and a long face that made her nose seem large. She had visible buck teeth.

I often will talk to people based solely on appearance. Everyone does it. I don't like to talk to people normally, but every once in a while I have a suspicion that someone might have something to say or be a good conversationalist.

"Hello," I said to her.

She looked at me with the expression that deer reserve for Mack trucks.

"Hello," she said.

"I'm Derwood," I said, using my joke nickname in case she turned out to be an utter psychotic.

"I'm Linda," she said.

"Are you a guest?" I asked.

"No, I'm one of the hosts," she said.

"Oh, you live here," I said.

"Yeah, I do," she said. "I guess that means you think I'm a slut?"

"Um, why?" I asked.

"Oh, everyone knows that the requirement for living here is that you sleep with the rest of the apartment," she said.

"Um," I said.

"Wow," said Lloyd. "And I thought they were loopy down at the Black Masses."

"I didn't know that," said John.

Charlie looked around and walked towards the front room.

The girl pulled in close to me.

"I'll fuck you now if you want," she said.

"Whoa!" said Lloyd.

"But I just got here," I protested.

John got a beer and walked after Charlie.

"Maybe you'd like your cock sucked?" she asked, moving down my front.

"Whoa, lady," I said. "I'm not interested, at least not with my girlfriend outside that door."

The girl looked up at me.

"Hey, I'll do you," said Lloyd. "But not in the kitchen."

"Come to my room," she said, grabbing Lloyd's hand.

"Hey, my lucky night," said Lloyd, as he was dragged down the hall by a girl about one hundred and fifty pounds lighter than him.

"You remain the champion of sleazy crap in my book, Lloyd," I shot after him They disappeared behind a door on the right about twenty feet down the main hallway.

"Wow," I said to myself as I grabbed a beer.

###

"Can we leave now?" asked Sam as she and Cathy walked back in.

"Did Cathy tell you what's so creepy?" I asked.

"Yeah," said Sam. "It's gross."

"That's not for you to judge," I said.

"For my own personal tastes, yes," she said. "The only people they could possibly attract with such a rule must be…"

"Really desperate to get laid?" asked Cathy, meaning it as a statement.

"Yeah," I said.

"Hey, where's Lloyd?" asked Sam.

At roughly the same time, the door twenty feet down the hall opened and Lloyd walked out. He was grinning smugly.

"Oh God," I said.

"Are you guys ready to go?" asked Lloyd. "'Cause I am."

Sam eyed Lloyd suspiciously.

"Let's leave then," I said. I suspected something amiss, and from Lloyd's tone I suspected it would enrage women.

"Where's Linda?" I asked.

"Washing her face," said Lloyd.

I bit my lip and grabbed Cathy's hand as I steered us down the hallway towards the front door. I looked behind us to make sure everyone was following — John, Lloyd, and Charlie were behind us. I looked around to spy Sam, and when I turned back Seth was standing between us and the door.

"Leaving so soon?" asked Seth. "What's the matter? Is it not good enough for you?"

"No, it was wonderful, Seth…" I began, and then a loud slam penetrated the hall.

"You son of a bitch!" shrieked Linda, appearing from nowhere behind Lloyd.

"What did you do to my girlfriend?" asked Seth, looking at all of us.

"Oh shit," I said.

"Gee, Seth," said Lloyd. "Linda here asked Derwood if she could suck his cock, so when he refused, I took over."

"What?" asked Seth.

"What about me?" screamed Linda, behind Lloyd.

"Does this happen everywhere, with him?" asked Sam, pointing at Lloyd.

"Only most of the time," I said. "Sometimes he surprises me."

"You need to calm down," said Lloyd.

"You got it all in my hair!" she said. "And my glasses are all smudgy now!"

"I can't believe this," said Seth.

"Can we go now?" asked Sam.

Seth looked at Sam and pulled out a gun.

"Not another gun!" I moaned.

Seth put the gun to his temple and pulled the trigger, spraying bright blood across the wall.

Sam looked at me.

Cathy looked at me.

Lloyd looked at me.

John looked at me.

Charlie looked at me.

Linda broke down screaming in hysterics.

"I guess the party's over," I said. I stepped over the ragdoll corpse of our host, and the others followed me across the threshold into the night air.

25

Learning to Dance Again

Hey Derwood," said Sam. I was sitting at my desk with my back to the door, and without looking I could tell that she had stuck -A- her head in our open door.

"Hello," I said as I studiously kept my attention on my email. "Come on in."

I heard Sam's footsteps behind me and she appeared in my field of view to the left, wearing a PVC skirt that caught my attention immediately.

"Where's Cathy?" she asked.

"At the doctor," I replied, not taking my eyes from the screen.

"Is she pregnant?" she asked. I turned and looked at her.

"What if she is?" I asked warily.

"I knew it!" squealed Sam.

"We're trying to figure out how to tell everyone," I said.

"I won't say a word," said Sam.

"Well, so far it's a secret between you, me and Cathy," I said.

"When is Cathy due back?" asked Sam.

"I'm not sure," I said. "She's been gone all day, she went at nine AM."

"Weird," said Sam, as the phone rang.

I picked up the phone to hear Cathy's voice crackling at me down the wires.

"Hey honey," she said. "I have to stay here at the hospital overnight."

"What?" I said, instantly alarmed.

"It's no big deal," she said. "They want to monitor me for a night while I sleep because of my asthma."

"No big deal?" I asked. "That's rather extreme for asthma."

"I'm serious, it's no big deal," she said, not convincing me. "This will help them treat it better as well."

"I love you," I said.

"I love you too, my love," she whispered back at me across the line.

I hung up the phone and looked at my screen for a second.

"You look like you need a beer," said Sam.

###

In the months since the shootings at the clubs, a number of small nightclubs had opened. Club owners shied away from hosting nights for people dressed in black, and a lot of the dark subculture died for a while. Raves became a constant menace.

A few clubs were so desperate that they began to have blackrock nights — changing the name to try and clear away the stigma associated with the word "goth". Small quiet affairs were held in bars that doubled as stranger genres by day, and Sam took me to one of these, a strange two-story bar on Polk Street. She was already dressed to go out, and I changed into clothes that were a little bit more presentable.

In my imagination, the tone of Polk Street hasn't changed much since they used it as a backdrop for a film adaptation of Frank Norris's 'Mc-Teague'. The street still is mostly residential flats above offices and shops, except now the grocery stores are open until three AM and the bars are probably a lot seedier.

The bar we went to was probably sculpted out of the interior of an old Victorian façade sometime in the seventies to make a nice fern bar. A rather nice bar looked like it might have come with the original building, and as we trudged up the stairs in our skirts, eyes wandered after us.

The money taker at the top of the stairs was a rather chipper young lady who seemed to know Sam, but then again, this wasn't surprising. Sam had much more of a social life than Cathy and I had. The thing that surprised me was that the money lady let us in for free, and told me that she'd heard a lot about me. Sam winked at me.

I sat down with a whiskey and coke, and surveyed my current surroundings. No decorations decorated the place, and from the inside the suggestion of a seventies disco strongly prevailed. A wooden dance floor ringed by mirrors had the stereotypical disco ball reflecting sickly light from a yellow filtered spotlight on it. I sat near the window, where I could pull back behind burgundy velvet curtains if spotted from the street. Sam deposited her stuff on the table and chairs.

"Do you dance?" she asked.

"No, not really," I said.

"Why not?" she asked.

"I never saw the point, really," I said.

"You never watched Cathy dance?" she asked.

"Well, yes, but I didn't start dating her for her dancing ability," I said. "I just don't get dancing."

"Huh," said Sam.

"What?" I asked.

"What don't you understand about it?" she asked.

"Well, I can understand the tapping of feet, and moving a little bit, but I've never figured out why people dance at all," I said.

"It seems obvious to me," said Sam.

"I'm a computer geek," I said. "I never really developed many social skills."

"I guess that could explain it, but I think you've just never really watched anyone dance," she said.

"What do you mean?" I asked.

"You never danced? Not even when you were a kid?"

"I did a long time ago," I said.

"How long?" she asked.

"The seventies," I said.

"Holy fuck," she said. "How old are you?"

"Don't you know?" I asked.

165

"No, never really cared," she said. "You're reasonably intelligent, so I don't know why it would matter before now… I just never imagined you'd have danced in the seventies…"

"I was six and I did 'The Bump' with a girl named Lisa. I can't remember her last name right now, but I'm sure I could if I had to." I said.

"Wow," said Sam. "The Bump. Is that that one where you knock asses together?"

"Yes," I replied, frostily.

"You seen anyone dance lately?" she asked me.

"Nope," I said.

"Well, gee, Derwood, watch me dance," she said as she pushed away from the table.

I tried to forget my girlfriend, who had told me not to bother to come visit her at the hospital, and tried to concentrate on watching Sam dance in front of me. She'd worn a rather severe-looking PVC corset that she was able to dance in despite the restrictions upon movement, and I tried to ignore the fact that she had fishnets on as I felt myself getting sweaty. Fishnets kill me, and Sam had the double whammy of being very shiny and wearing fishnets.

In retrospect, I don't even remember many of the songs the deejay was playing. I sat in my seat and drank. The bar didn't even have a booth for the deejay, and I thought the deejay was a woman until I approached her to ask for a song. It turned out that the deejay was either transgender or a transvestite — she had the deep voice and Adam's apple that marked her for a him, plus the chesty effect she was going for had been achieved with a lot of foam padding. I requested something by Covenant and wandered back to my seat to watch Sam.

Sam and I had lived together for many months at this point, and I thought I'd gotten to know her pretty well. I realized I was wrong after watching her dance. I can't really describe it any better than that I felt like I was taking a peek at someone else's soul. Not much ever makes me feel like that.

She started out the evening doing a graceful repeating dance that started with her arms moving in waves around her body as it swayed around. She traced a circuitous route across the empty dance floor and stepped in time to every other beat of the music as she undulated her torso around. The effect was rather erotic and I got kind of disturbed that I was watching my roommate dance suggestively while my pregnant girlfriend was in the hospital.

I drank steadily while Sam danced, and before I realized it the bartender was announcing last call and a very sweaty Sam was dragging me to a cab waiting for us downstairs.

The next thing I clearly remember was standing on the doorstep with Sam at the house, looking at a piece of paper tacked to the front door.

"Lloyd's at the hospital," I heard Sam say from what seemed like a million miles away. Why had I drunk so much?

"What happened to Lloyd?" I asked in my drunken stupor.

"Lloyd wrote the note," said Sam. "He's fine. Something is wrong with Cathy."

I sobered up at that precise instant.

###

I've never adequately found words to describe what happened to me when I found out about Cathy's death. I felt so detached at the time, which some will attribute to the alcohol coursing through my veins. I was completely sober, however, and can remember the details with great clarity. I knew that something was horribly wrong the instant Sam had read the note to me, and all I was doing until I arrived at the hospital was sitting there numbly telling myself that it wasn't happening and it couldn't possibly be happening.We walked into the lobby of the hospital on Geary sometime after three AM, and found Lloyd, John and Charlie sitting in the lobby waiting for us. At about that time, the sensation hit me.

The sensation in question was a hot, buzzing feeling that washed over my body like a warm wave. I had never experienced going into shock before, and I started to get lightheaded. Sweat broke out on my forehead and I grabbed a chair to support myself.

Lloyd and Sam lead me into a stainless steel elevator that was abnormally large. I suddenly realized it was to hold gurneys, and that it went all the way to the basement where the morgue was.

We didn't go down — we went up.

When we got to the fifth floor, I was led into a hallway that looked and smelled like every other hallway — white surfaces reflecting fluores-cents, a bleached smell that covered some faint malignant odor. I found myself in a small office behind a nursing station and in front of a doctor who was talking to me. The buzzing sensation had become a violent sound by this point. When I heard the words telling me that she was dead, I felt blackness close in and the buzzing grew worse until I closed my eyes and forced myself back to coherency.

"Do you understand me?" he asked. "We tried everything we could."

I shook my head no. I couldn't comprehend it at that moment. I'd spent almost every waking hour of the past four years of my life in her presence or at least within five minutes of her. We'd never been separated longer than the hours I worked and when she'd gone to Los Angeles, and I had happily assumed I would be spending the rest of my life without being separated from her for much longer than that.

I'd spent the past few hours at a bar, drinking and getting horny over my roommate while my girlfriend and child lay dying in a hospital for miles away, robbed of their breath and turning blue. I'd stumbled home drunkenly as they covered her face with a sheet, and the last thing she had ever said to me was something about how it was nothing and I should go have fun while they checked her out at the hospital.

We rode the elevator again, and the buzzing seemed louder. I watched the lights on the floor indicator retreating downward and my heart hit bottom at about the same time the indicator marked "B" lit up.

I watched from a thousand miles away as they removed the sheet from her face, and I saw her in an instant as the perfect creature I remembered and had never seen since I had first fallen in love with her. She looked peaceful and as if she were only asleep, except that her face, neck and lips were a bluish gray color. I realized the tears had been falling from my face onto the blood gutters in the gurney, and that I probably was going to be able to fill them with no problem.

My girlfriend and child were dead. I wanted to be responsible for it, I felt guilty, and in the end I was left as I had come into this world - - cold, confused and very alone. I withdrew so far into myself that I was completely unaware of Lloyd, Sam, John and Charlie cramming me into a cab home.

26

Lloyd's Satanic Clubhouse

I poured the contents of the cardboard carton into the sea at the ruined base of the Golden Gate Bridge as Sam and John and Lloyd looked on. She hadn't wanted to be put into the sea at this spot, but Cathy would have understood - she had been there when her favorite spot had been wiped out by the big waves.

I still felt numb. It made it better to pour her ashes out into the waiting sea, but I kept a small vial full of them on an antique silver chain. The mortuary refused my request for her skull.

I had the satisfaction of a good answer to someone who sneered "Whose funeral?" at me.

Other than these things, I was generally miserable.

###

"Hey, man," said Lloyd as I wandered into the kitchen one Sunday morning.

"What?" I answered out of my haze.

"You've been like this for months," he said.

"What month is it?" I asked.

"July," he said.

"That's when the baby would have been born," I said.

"I didn't know about that," said Lloyd.

"I know you didn't," I said. "It's just starting to be a little more real to me."

"I hate it when that happens," said Lloyd.

"Yeah, me too," I said.

"Wow, that's the first joke I heard you crack since that whole skull thing with the mortuary," said Lloyd.

"I wasn't joking," I said.

"Oh," said Lloyd. "About the skull?"

"Yeah," I said.

"I actually think I understand that," he said.

"Understand what?" said Sam as she walked in.

"Never mind, Sam," I said.

Sam stopped dead in her tracks and looked at me.

"You just spoke to me," she said.

"I haven't spoken to you?" I asked.

"Not in a while," she said. "I was starting to get really worried about you."

"I'm fine," I said.

"I'm glad," she said. "I was pretty shaken up too."

"I can imagine you've had a shitty year as well," I said.

"You can say that again," she sighed.

"Where is everyone else?" I asked.

"John is at work, so is Charlie," said Sam.

"I think I want to take a walk," I said.

"You want to be alone?" asked Sam.

"I don't care," I said.

"Hey, if you're going towards the Haight I have a meeting to go to," said Lloyd.

Sam and I looked at Lloyd.

"Okay," I said. "I'm going to Golden Gate Park."

###

We came to a stop in front of a large statue outside the entrance to the California Academy of Sciences. Cathy and I first encountered this statue on a trip to the museum to see an exhibit on bats. As I stood in front of the statue, standing in nearly the same spot where we had held each other once, I felt tears coming out of my eyes. The numbness of the past weeks had vanished, and I felt the pain sear through me like the afterthought of a scalpel that cut through emotions. Lloyd and Sam stood beside me quietly as I felt the pain and hurt turn to something akin to pure rage.

"Lloyd," I said.

"Yeah, man," said Lloyd, coming into view on my right.

"I know the answer," I said.

"To what?" he asked.

"The statues," I said.

"Aw, man!" said Lloyd. "Don't you get it by now?"

"Yes," I said.

"No you don't," said Lloyd, exasperated. "I made all that shit up."

"Then how did everyone else know about it?" I asked.

"Like who?" he asked.

"Charlie knew," I said.

"Right," said Sam. "And the landlord knew."

"Right," I said. "And I know you were making it all up, Lloyd."

"Huh?" asked Sam and Lloyd, at the same time.

"This entire thing has been a spell in action," I said.

"What do you mean?" asked Lloyd.

"Yes," I said. "This was all started by a bunch of guys back around the turn of the century. They didn't even know what they were doing. They decided to just put these statues in a pentagram and see what happened. I'm sure of it."

"Then what do you think happened?" asked Lloyd.

"Chaos," I said.

"Explain," said Sam.

"By leaving their 'spell' open-ended like that," I said, "They gave it a life of its own. They planted enough rumors to start the urban legend and that was it."

"So," said Lloyd," are you telling me that the people that kept the rumors alive…"

"…were defining the parameters of the spell," I finished. "The spell is the sum of everything that has ever been said about it."

"Shit," said Lloyd.

"We can use this," I said.

"How?" asked Lloyd.

"I have to figure it out," I said.

I started to walk towards the Shakespeare Garden. Lloyd and Sam scurried after me, and I continued to talk as I walked.

"There's only one thing I want enough to warp a one-hundred year old Chaos spell to my own nefarious purposes," I said.

"You can't possibly be thinking what I'm thinking," said Lloyd.

"Yes," I said. "I want Cathy back."

"Derwood, honey," Sam said, taking my hand and forcing me to stop. "Dead's dead. Cathy isn't coming back."

"We have to try!" I nearly shouted. "The alternative is too much to bear! I can't stop thinking it, because if I say it we're all completely and utterly fucked!"

Sam grabbed me and held me close. I broke into a hiccupping moan that was the best I could do to manage crying at the moment. I realized that I had cried so much my eyes were dry.

"You can just say nothing, okay?" she asked. "Please do that, for me. We're all really stressed ourselves."

"How can I live without her?" I sobbed.

"I don't know," sighed Sam. "I miss her too. We just have to find a way."

I sobbed there for a while, and as I did I felt the same rage build up inside of me. This time, I kept quiet about it. In my head I began to plot.

###

"So, these people are kind of nervous," said Lloyd as we walked up to the front of an ominous hunter green Victorian. All the heavy looking curtains seemed to be drawn.

"Like how?" asked Sam. "Drug paranoid?"

"Not exactly," said Lloyd. "More like pituitary paranoid."

"I won't ask," I said.

Lloyd pressed the doorbell.

We waited a minute. I noticed the small round ball of a small computer cam tucked in one corner of the porch near the ceiling.

Lloyd pressed the doorbell again.

The door slowly creaked open, and a woman peered out at us. Most of her body was obscured behind the door, and she looked like she hadn't seen sunlight in several years. Her hair was straight, long, and bright purple. Her face was round with a button nose accenting the middle of it.

"Yeah?" she asked. "Hey Lloyd. Who are your friends?"

"This is my roommate Sam, and this is my roommate Derwood," said Lloyd. "I told you about them before. Guys, this is Wanda."

"Oh yeah," said the woman. "Come on in. Nice to meet you."

The door opened wider, and I saw that she was wearing a black t-shirt. It had a smiling pig in a police outfit, and below it in large letters was a slogan - HOW'S YOUR PORK? She was smaller than any of us, yet she had a very full figure.

"Likewise," I said. I instantly surveyed the inside of the house. The first thing anyone who walks into a San Francisco Victorian should do is look at the interior decoration. This Victorian was no different.

Most of the houses people normally associate with San Francisco were actually built from kits around the turn of the century. As such, they all follow the same basic layout. This house was about four stories, with the same type of cupola our house had. The cupola was on the other side of the façade than our cupola, and the foyer opened upon a staircase and a living room that Wanda ushered us into.

The windows looked like the curtains had been drawn from the outside. On the inside, I could see that half-inch steel plating draped in velvet had been bolted over the windows.

Wanda turned towards me.

"I'd like to offer my condolences for your girlfriend," she said in a formal tone. "Lloyd told me about what happened, he was shaken up as any good friend would be."

"Thank you," I said numbly. "We were all surprised."

Wanda looked a little uncomfortable for a second, her eyes darting around nervously. Lloyd was next to a mantelpiece inspecting a candleholder.

"If I might ask," she began, "exactly how did she die? Lloyd was a bit fuzzy about that."

How had Cathy died? The past few months were a vague blur to me, but I found that I knew the answer as if it had been recorded onto my frontal lobes with a branding iron.

"She had asthma," I said. "She got pregnant, and the pregnancy made the asthma kick into high gear. She went in for a check-up once, and during a test she started to have an attack. They decided to keep her overnight, and in the middle of the night she woke up to a severe asthma attack and her rescue inhaler wouldn't work. She'd been overusing it."

"Oh geez," said Wanda. "I'm so sorry."

"It's not your fault," I said. "Death just happens."

"That doesn't make it any easier," said Sam from across the room. I looked up to see her holding a skull.

"So when is the fun?" asked Lloyd.

"Always the icebreaker, huh, Lloyd?" asked Wanda.

"I just love talking about things that drive barbs into the hearts of my friends and roommates," said Lloyd wryly. Wanda grew silent.

"What fun is this?" asked Sam. "Can Derwood and I participate in fun?" Wanda looked at her, first up and then down.

"You'd make a good altar," she said. "We're setting up in the basement, Lloyd."

"Hoo-ray," said Lloyd, and he moved towards the foyer.

"You two can watch," said Wanda. "Whatever you do, don't talk."

Wanda moved after Lloyd.

"What the fuck is she talking about?" whispered Sam as she sidled up to me and grabbed my arm.

"I think we're about to witness a Black Mass," I said.

"Oh great, what about the altar comment?" she hissed.

"Virgin sacrifice, symbolic of course," I said. "Basically you lie there on the slab and get fucked by all the members of the 'coven.'"

"Good god, how boring," she said. "Is this what sexually deprived people do in their spare time?"

"Well, Lloyd does it," I said as I reached the stairs.

"Touché, " said Sam.

We felt our way into the blackness of the stairwell. An eerie red light beckoned us to the bottom of the stairs, and we could see a rough concrete floor waiting for us there. The walls had been painted black.

"Have you ever seen one of these?" asked Sam.

"Nope," I said.

We reached the end of the stairs and walked into a large open basement area. Heavy black fabric covered the walls, and there were candles in large standing wrought iron holders everywhere. There was a giant pentagram (pentacle? Which way was up?) inscribed on the floor, and in the middle of it was a table draped with more black fabric. As we got down there, we saw that Wanda was stripping.

"Nice ass," said Sam.

"Shhh," said Lloyd. We hadn't seen him because he had put on a black robe and blended in with the walls. As our eyes adjusted to the red light, we noticed that there were about ten other men and women lined against the walls. They all had black robes on, and the women were wearing large strap-on dildos.

When Wanda was nude, she lay upon the altar. One of the men, a particularly coarse-looking man who was a little more heavyset than Lloyd, stepped forward.

"We need absolute silence," he said.

Almost immediately, Wanda started floating.

"Whoa," said Sam.

"Whoa!" said the Satanists.

"I'm fairly sure that's not supposed to happen," I said.

"Really?" asked Sam.

Wanda flopped onto the table and sat up with her back to us. I felt the room grow cold, and the Satanists scrambled for the stairs. Lloyd just kind of stood there with his mouth open. This was something I could deal with—if it made Lloyd's jaw drop, it was some fairly heavy shit.

"Derwood, let's get out of here," said Sam. "This is really fucked up."

"Let's collect Lloyd first," I said.

I started to move towards Lloyd as the Satanists stampeded past Sam and me. The candles suddenly extinguished themselves, and we were left bathed in the red light from the colored bulb that was lighting the basement.

I stopped dead in my tracks as I heard a cracking sound. I saw Wanda's head turn around to stare at me, and I realized that the sound was that of her vertebrae snapping as her head twisted on its neck.

"Hello, worm," said Wanda in a voice that was completely unlike the voice we'd heard her speak in upstairs. This voice was as if someone had taken a cheese grater and rubbed it on the vocal cords of a person with throat cancer. She was looking straight at me.

"Hi there," I said. "How's it going?"

Lloyd guffawed. Sam squeaked a little bit.

"Let's cut the crap," said Wanda.

"OK, let's," I said. "Who are you? I don't think you're Wanda."

"I am TUTIVILLUS," said Wanda.

"Oh, demon of nit-picking," I said.

"Silence!" said TUTIVILLUS.

"Make me," I said.

"Your Cathy is comfortable with us," he said.

"You shut the fuck up," I said.

"Make me," said TUTIVILLUS.

"Point taken," I said. "What makes you think Cathy is with you?"

"Everyone who dies here descends to the next level," he said.

"Excuse me?" I asked.

"You humans are really stupid," said TUTIVILLUS. "Your city exists on a plane between the physical and the realm in which I dwell."

"Shit," said Lloyd.

"No, that's another plane," said TUTIVILLUS.

"So why have you come here and now?" I asked. "Why not upstairs in the foyer? Why not at the height of the ceremony?"

"I do what I want," said TUTIVILLUS.

"Yeah," I said. "Sure you do."

"Look, do you want to hear what I have to say or not?" asked TUTIVILLUS.

"You've already told me a lot," I said.

"I've been watching you. I've been watching you through the statues. I see everything that they see," said TUTIVILLUS.

"So what?" I asked. "What does that have to do with me?"

"Don't fuck with the statues," said the thing speaking from Wanda. "You may think that you know what you're doing, but you have no idea."

"Wouldn't dream of it," I said.

"Good," said TUTIVILLUS, and then Wanda flopped over. Lloyd got to her first.

"She's dead," he said, checking her pulse.

"Broken neck will do that," I said.

"OK, this has passed beyond fucked up," said Sam. "What the fuck did that all mean?"

"Isn't it obvious, Sam?" I asked. "That thing confirmed something I knew all along."

"What's that?" asked Sam.

"I live in Hell," I said.

Sam and Lloyd and I stood in the basement with Wanda's cooling corpse, wondering what in San Francisco to do next.

27

The Fog

An unspecified amount of bomb-making material was taken from the Lawrence Livermore Lab," blared the television as we walked in the front door. John was sprawled on the couch with his hand firmly shoved down the front of his pants, probably whacking off to the evening news.

"What the fuck is a neutron bomb?" asked John at us.

"What?" asked Sam.

"Neutron bomb," said Charlie, coming in from the direction of the kitchen. "Kills people but leaves buildings standing."

"Rock on, Charlie, you're becoming as morbid as we are," said Lloyd.

"Naw," said Charlie. "I just remember that one because it scares the piss out of me."

"Yeah, it sounds like a nasty way to die," said Lloyd. "High level radiation flash that boils your skin off and dissipates rapidly."

"Well, someone's stolen the materials to make one," said John.

"You've never heard of the neutron bomb?" I asked.

"No," said John.

"They're urging everyone to stay indoors," said Sam, pointing at the television. "What a bunch of dumbasses."

"Yeah," said Lloyd. "At least with a nuclear bomb you can halfway rationalize fantasies about the blast shadow of some solid marble building or something. What the fuck good will staying indoors do?"

"Whatever," I said. "It just goes to show that our parents were pure evil. Why even keep stuff like that around? I think I need a beer."

"I need a joint," said John.

Sam sat down on the couch and pulled a blanket over herself. "I need a rest."

"I need a movie," said Lloyd. "Anyone want to watch something?"

I padded through the swinging door to the kitchen and mused over neutron bombs while I reached into the refrigerator. Growing up with the constant threat of nuclear terror in the mid-eighties made me extremely blasé about the entire affair – who cared? We're all going to be incinerated by the radiation blast someday, might as well enjoy ourselves. Someone stole a neutron bomb. How droll.

I walked back in to the living room to see Lloyd popping a videotape into the VCR. John lit up a joint he'd pulled from somewhere, and I sat down next to Sam, closest to the windows in the front living room.

Everyone started watching the movie. I watched outside the window as I took hits on the joint that was going around. The movie playing was a giant comet/asteroid movie from the previous summer, featuring whooshing spaceships and cowboys dressed in pressure suits. I ignored it as hard as I could. I watched the streetlights outside burn with the clarity of sodium, and car headlights reflected onto the buildings across the street.

They discovered the large hunk of space rock hurtling towards the earth in the first five minutes of the movie. Everyone stared at the screen as the bad news was relayed from person to person all the way up to the President of the United States, a suave looking man who grimly decided to draw up all plans to destroy the thing. About the time that the President received word of the space rock, the first tendrils of fog started to drift into the city from the sea.

People in San Francisco tend to take fog for granted. It drifts in almost every night during the summer, lazily floating in from the sea through the streets towards downtown. It takes on an interesting appearance as it does this – you can watch fogbanks roll in over buildings, and envelope them like a wave of smothering milk. In streets that run perpendicular to the sea, you can watch as it slowly creeps by you like a live thing.

I watched as the fog rolled in. The escapades on the small screen were a million miles away from me. I thought about neutron bombs and TUTIVILLUS. I thought about pentagrams and Satanists. I thought about Cathy. Billowing clouds of vapor flowed past the front window, and I felt tears come to my eyes as I remembered the hole in my heart.

I watched the fog roll by, and saw shapes in it. Could that be?

Sam pushed the blanket over me, and pushed herself into my side. I was distracted from watching the fog by this, and I took my head away, looking down at her head nestling in my shoulder.

"Do you mind?" she asked. I thought about this for a small while.

"No," I sighed. "Just don't expect anything more than an emotional void."

"Ain't we all, sweetie," said Sam quietly, and she scrunched down a little bit more to watch the movie.

I looked back outside the front window. The fog sailed past, forming and reforming in to strange blobs. It all looked like normal fog, but for some reason the fog was different. It was something to be felt and smelled, like fear. I could feel it smothering the house.

Sam moved her hand and took mine into it.

"I'm here for you, you know?" she asked.

"Yes," I said. "I know."

"I thought I'd never say that to you and have you understand," she said. "I just wanted to tell you while you understood me."

John glared at Sam, and Lloyd turned around from his position on the floor. Sam hugged my arm, and became silent again.

I turned my attention back to outside the window.

Tendrils of fog caressed the trellises of the Victorian façade on the house. If I looked at them just right, I could see ghostly shapes in them, elongated limbs and strange wriggling masses. Either the marijuana John was passing around was laced with something, or I just wasn't used to smoking pot in a while. I was trying to figure out exactly which when I saw it. There was no mistaking it, either. As I stared out the window at the fogbank moving slowly past, a face came sharply into focus and looked straight up at me.

It was a man, and his disembodied face had hollow eyesockets above gaunt cheekbones. His mouth was hanging slack-jawed, as if it were a corpse. Below his mouth, the neck faded into an amorphous blob that I realized was part of the fogbank.The face lolled and faded back into the fogbank, and the shape of its torso, legs and feet moved underneath the outer layer of fog.

I might have gasped at this, but then I noticed that the entire fogbank was writhing with vague shapes like feet, arms, hands and shoulders. I slowly moved Sam away from me, and as she felt the pressure she sat up a little bit. I escaped from underneath her and moved towards the front window.

I felt the eyes of the others on my back as I walked towards the front window. I stared out at the slowly moving cloud, and felt the hair on the back of my neck stand straight on end.

"Yo, Derwood, what's up?" asked Lloyd.

I wasn't the only person interested in the fog. As I watched, our landlord slowly walked out of his apartment and stared up at the lumpy cloud moving down the street. His face had a combination of pure astonishment and joy on it. He looked like he was looking at porn.

"Well, that's pretty fucked up," I said.

"What?" asked Charlie. "Something weird happening?"

"I'm not sure," I said. "It might be the pot, but I swear I saw a face in the cloud. An d the landlord is seeing shit in the fog too, he's out here."

"Oh, you're just crazy," said Charlie. "Only crazy people see shit in the fog."

"Charlie!" exclaimed Sam.

I looked out the window into the fogbank, and saw Cathy's face staring back at me.

"Yeah, you're right," I said. "I'm not feeling well."

Lloyd got up and walked towards me.

"What you seeing?" he asked. "Bodies in the fog? Disembodied faces? Severed limbs?"

I nodded, slowly.

"Shit," he said. "I see that kind of thing all the time in the fog. Depends on how much acid I did that night."

The landlord looked up, and noticed us in the window. He smiled up at us, and pointed at the fogbank.

"Isn't it beautiful?" he shouted.

"Yeah," I mouthed.

"Fucking crazies," muttered Lloyd.

I walked out onto the porch and watched the fog flowing by, faster and thicker. The pressure of discorporate bodies made me feel as if I were walking through molasses, and I realized that whatever was happening, it was starting to pick up.

"It's fun to watch this process everyday," intoned the landlord. "The fog wraps its way through the streets to caress the heart of the city. It's awe inspiring."

"What?" I said.

"To the center," said the landlord. "First to the center and then across towards where the city began."

"The fog?" I asked.

"Yes," he said. "It is a part of the mystery of this place."

"I know that," I said testily. "I've been here a while, I'm not a tourist anymore. Stop dicking with me and tell me what you see in the fog."

"Dammit," I added.

"OK," he said. "I see faces, and body parts. Kinda like serial killer porn."

"So what does it mean?" I asked. "Why am I seeing the same thing?"

"Maybe you're starting to see the world for what it really is," he said.

"Why did I see Cathy's face?" I asked.

"Well, then, maybe you're just a little crazy," he said to me brightly. "She died right? My condolences."

"What does it mean?" I asked.

"Why does it have to 'mean' something?" asked the landlord. "It's chaos. Fog is the epitome of chaos – it swirls and forms and rolls around in unpredictable ways. It's so beautiful…"

"I just need to find something to hang onto," I said softly. "This is all too much."

"Just let go," he said. "Always pick the methods of maximum destruction."

"What?" I asked.

"We all have our destiny," said the landlord. "Remember, everything each of us does is in the best interest of the human race, no matter what. I cull the herd. You know why?"

I shook my head no.

"It's because the only way to get remembered," he said, "the only way is to get on the news, to get your place in the history books by organizing huge slaughters. Jeffrey Dahmer, look at him. Look at Hitler. Look at Stalin. You want to be remembered forever? Kill a whole fuckload of people at once. All this peace and love bullshit, it's stupid."

"I want to live forever," said the landlord.

"Um, ok," I said. "I'm going back inside now."

"Goodnight," said the landlord.

28

Cadaver Tank Redux

Your problem," said Sam, "Is that you can only see your own point of view."

"Not exactly," said Lloyd. "It's just that I choose not to see yours."

It was 10am on Sunday morning. I'd gotten up at about nine, as I did everyday. Out of sheer boredom I started making pancakes. I hadn't made pancakes in a long time – they'd been a favorite of Cathy's. Everyone was woken up by the smell, and at about nine-thirty, a crowd of roommates had stumbled into the kitchen snipping at each other before they'd had their morning coffee.

"Cut it out, you guys," said Charlie. Charlie's mother had moved out while I wasn't looking, taking her foul smelling herbs with her. I was secretly happy, but it was probably the least of my worries.

"What were you guys arguing about again?" I asked.

"Fate versus determinism," said John. "Boring and juvenile stuff, try a real debate."

"Why are we redoing all the old arguments?" I asked. "Why don't we try to break some new ground?"

"Why?" asked John. "What good will it do?"

I looked around at all of them.

"I just want this to be over," I said.

"What do you mean?" asked Lloyd.

"I'm just wondering how anything can get any weirder," I said. "I'm making pancakes for a Satanist, a mooch, and a girl that does internet porn. Cathy is dead, the city I love is in ruins, and it seems like it's the end of the world, or at least we've fallen into some nebulous layer of hell. Where does it end? What's the point?"

"We don't know," said Sam. "We're just trying to live here."

"Why?" I asked.

"I don't think we really know that either," said Lloyd. "I mean, we try to pretend, but it's all pretty pointless, don't you think?"

"But we never talk about this sort of thing," I said. "We never try to figure anything out."

"You do," said Sam. "You do so much it makes my brain hurt."

The pain was sharp. Why did that bother me?

"What's wrong with thinking?" I asked.

"You did it so much you never appreciated Cathy," she said quietly. The room grew deathly still.

"There's no call for that," I said quietly.

"Yeah, whoa, chill," said Lloyd. "We're having pancakes."

Slowly, anger built inside of me as I thought about what she'd said. I flipped a pair of pancakes and turned my back until I composed myself. I wiped away a tear with an oven mitt.

Sam sat down quietly, and no one said anything for what seemed like weeks.

###

I wondered for a while if Sam understood how badly her words had hurt me. It must have been bad if Lloyd had told her to chill. She didn't acknowledge me, however, and this stung even more.

I usually refer to the words of Ambrose Bierce when considering apologies. Mr. Bierce was a major reason I moved to San Francisco. I figured that if they had put up with this guy, they could put up with me as well. He wrote a book that was popular amongst systems administrators a long time ago.

There used to be a program on computers called 'fortune', as in 'fortune cookie'. This program was simple – it merely picked a random line out of a file and displayed it. The contents of the file were the real treat. Files existed with sayings from popular cartoons, x-rated sayings, and the file that introduced me to Mr. Bierce – a copy of his acclaimed 'Devil's Dictionary'. He defined apologies thusly:

Apologize: To lay the groundwork for a future offense.

Meaning that I didn't expect an apology from her, but I wouldn't mind being talked to. The basic thing behind apology is to give an excuse not to work through problems – to let each other off the hook and not talk out something. Lloyd and John didn't dare mention it around me, and I slowly realized that everyone in the house was waiting for me to talk to Sam before feeling good about anything.

Why had she said something like that? I couldn't fathom her brain. I realized that I didn't know her as well as I thought, even though I'd seen her daily for almost a year. We all stayed to ourselves most of the time, and I really had never spent a lot of time with her. I drew back trying to think of something to say. If I talked to her about it, would she attack me about Cathy again? It hurt me again to hear Sam's implication that maybe I didn't love my girlfriend as much as I should have.

Why did I even care? What point was there to any of this?

###

I finally talked to Sam the night we found out that John had been arrested for trafficking in human body parts. I answered the phone call.

"Hello?" I asked.

"Derwood, man," came John's voice over the line. "The Feds took us, man. Me and the doctors. They closed down the tank, man."

"How awful," I said.

"Don't worry, I didn't give them my address," he said. "No way to trace me back to you."

"What about this phone call?" I asked.

Silence on the other end of the line, and then John swore.

"Shit, I am so fucking stupid," he said.

"Don't worry, we're on it," I said.

I hung up the phone after a little bit. The Feds had taken John and the doctors to Sacramento and a federal holding facility there – they evidently had thought that maybe someone in San Francisco would try to bail them out was what John's attorney had said. The medical center had a very expensive attorney retained for this, John said. This was just part of his job and he was sure they would compensate him for it. I didn't have the heart to tell John that he was taking the fall for over ninety years of bad management decisions.

I nearly ran into Sam in the hallway outside the bathroom. We stood there and stared at each other for a second.

Whenever I first meet someone, I look at their face and try to imprint it on my mind. I had met Sam a long time ago, but I relished every chance to look at her face and notice something new about it. It was part of the fun of being around people, I figured. I could recall Cathy's face very clearly in my mind due to this habit – I'd watched her sleep on countless insomniac nights. I looked at Sam's face and saw something new in it. I couldn't put my finger on it, but I mouthed the words anyway.

"I was angry at you for thinking I was bad to Cathy," I said. "I couldn't help it. I haven't been calm enough to tell you until now."

"I was wrong to say that," said Sam. "It was what I was feeling at the time, but I realize that I don't know you very well and I had no right to say that."

"It's done," I said. "In the past. We need to clean out John's room of any body parts he might have up there"

"What?" asked Sam.

"I hate to have to shift gears on you here, but John was pinched by the FBI for trafficking in human body parts, and we've got to get rid of that hand he's got."

"Shit fucking goddamn it," said Sam.

"Yeah," I agreed.

We hurried up the stairway onto the second floor, and opened the door to John's room. What we saw there horrified us.

Human arms stacked like cordwood. Feet in a row in a shoe rack. Two heads sat in a bag on his desk. In the midst of it all was the Hand of Glory.

"Holy fuck," said Lloyd, sticking his head in.

"Landlord," said Sam.

"What?" I asked.

"He'd know how to get rid of all of this," said Sam as she turned to me.

###

We stood behind the landlord as he sized it all up.

"Back way," he said. "We'll take it down to my apartment in the back way."

"What?" I said. "They'll have a search warrant!"

"For a specific room, you friend's room," said the landlord. "Look, the law is very specific here. They have to have a warrant to search the suspect's room, nobody else's. A room is defined as a room with a lock on the door."

He batted at the padlock and hasp on John's door.

"It'll be safe in my apartment."

"Creepy," said Lloyd. "Why not just use the Hand of Glory?"

"What?" I asked.

"That stuff doesn't work," said Sam.

"Why not try it?" asked Lloyd. "I want to see if it works anyways. We could take everything down the front and we'd be safe."

"No, let's not risk it," said the landlord.

"Come on, we could get caught and then you'd be famous!" said Lloyd. The landlord twitched.

Lloyd picked up the board holding the hand of glory and produced a lighter in one hand.

"No, don't," said the landlord weakly.

"Tell you what," said Lloyd as he lit the pinky finger.

"Let me try this," and the ring finger was lit.

189

"We'll see what happens," the middle finger flickered alight and sputtered fat.

"And you won't be responsible," the index finger came to life.

"For anything that happens," said Lloyd and then the thumb was fully lit.

I looked at the flame until Lloyd blew it out. We all shook our heads.

The room was clean.

"Stacked like cordwood in the basement," said Lloyd. "I put your keys back in your pocket, landlord dude."

"What the fuck?" said Sam.

"Hand of Glory is cool," said Lloyd. "It was originally a tool for thieves. You light it, and everyone in your target house is asleep. That book tells me that it affects the mind of anyone who sees it, except for the person holding the board there."

"Wicked," said the landlord.

"Don't even think about it," said Lloyd. "It goes in my room."

"Well, why was it in that book?" I asked.

"Isn't it obvious?" asked Lloyd.

"No, what?" I asked. Sam stood next to me.

"They used them so they could work undisturbed," he said. "So they could desecrate the statues."

"What do you think is happening?" I asked.

"Well, I know exactly one thing," said Lloyd. "Whatever is happening has gone too far to stop."

I nodded my head in agreement.

"So now, we just have to figure out how to finish it," I said.

"Well, if the Hand of Glory works," I said, "then maybe we should start reading that book a lot more."

The landlord excused himself, and we each retired to our rooms.

###

I laid in bed thinking about the hollow spot next to me when my door creaked open on rusty hinges.

190

Sam didn't say a word as she crept into the oversized bed, pressed herself against me, and kissed my cheek goodnight. We fell asleep that way, and it warmed me to think of the other time that Sam had fallen asleep in the bed I'd shared with Cathy. I think we both felt a little better.

29

Tour De Force

W hat're we gonna do with John's car?" asked Sam.

John's car was beginning to be a problem. I had to move it every few days to avoid getting tickets, and with John away the vandals were starting to pick at the tiny diorama of a graveyard that he'd built on the VW's outer skin. A quick check of all the controls revealed that it was a stick shift, which nobody knew how to drive except for me.

Lloyd, Sam and I sat in the kitchen around cups of coffee as we tried to figure out what to do next. Life in the house had gone about as far downhill as we could bear. Our numbers were being whittled down one by one, and whoever was left probably was going to be fodder for our serial-murdering landlord.

"What's up, guys?" asked Charlie as he bounced into the room.

"Not much, Charlie," I said.

"I wanted to tell you, I'm moving out soon," said Charlie. "Mom has the flat fixed now."

We all looked up.

"That's cool," said Sam.

"Yeah," said Lloyd.

"Actually, she's been asking me for months," he said quietly. "I just didn't want to leave. I've been having fun."

We all looked up, this time in shock.

"Wow," I said.

"Yeah, go figure," said Lloyd.

"What's going on?" asked Charlie.

"We're trying to figure out what to do with John's car," said Sam.

###

We stood at the curb with keys we'd found in John's desk on a VW key fob. We first searched the car to make sure it was clear of body parts, then settled into the interior and meditated on what to do next. Lloyd insisted on sitting in the passenger seat and sitting up straight so his head went through the sun roof. I fiddled with my police band scanner – I'd gotten even more attached to it since I thought that Federal agents might be raiding the house.

"Wow, this is nice," said Charlie.

"You've got to be kidding me," said Lloyd.

"Where do we want to go?" I asked. "I vote we rent a storage space and store this fucker."

"Sounds good to me," said Sam from the back.

"I'll pitch in for that, John can pay us back," said Lloyd.

"Where do we go?" asked Sam.

"Third Street," I said. "I know a storage place there."

I shifted the car into first and pulled away from the curb. A couple of turns and we were on Haight Street heading downhill.

"Out of the way," I growled at other cars. I don't like driving in the city.

It was Charlie that first noticed them.

"Do you think we're being followed?" asked Charlie.

I looked in the rear view mirrors and saw a black Mercedes following us.

"Someone is stuck behind us, Charlie," I said.

"Try turning," said Lloyd.

"Okay," I said. "Here."

I turned right onto Fillmore Street, towards Duboce Triangle Park. The Mercedes signaled and turned with us.

"They're still behind us," I reported.

"Stop at this stop sign," said Lloyd.

"Okay," I said as we slowed to a stop.

Lloyd opened the door and got out.

At almost the same time as Lloyd, three doors on the Mercedes opened up and three Asian men in severe black suits and sunglasses got out.

"Fuck!" yelled Charlie.

"What?" I asked. "Triad? Who are these people!"

"My brothers!" yelled Charlie. "Get back in the car, go go go!"

Lloyd hopped back in the car and I popped the clutch, squealing the tires and slamming the passenger door shut. The three men looked confused for a second, then jumped back into the car as they started to pursue us. I squealed into Germania Street and gunned it towards Webster Street, hoping to round the corner there before they could see where I went to.

We dodged pedestrians and bicyclists as we shot out of Webster back onto Haight Street. I decided to take it up and use the Volkswagen's natural affinity to be a complete and utter rock to shoot me down the hill from Haight Street to Market Street.

I had one advantage over the men in the shiny black Mercedes – I had no compunctions about what the car looked like after this ride.

We shot down Haight Street into the section that turned into a one way street as it went under the Cypress Freeway.

"Whoa, shit," screamed Lloyd. "Fuckin' Steve McQueen in a Beetle !"

Sam was laughing maniacally in the backseat, while Charlie was quiet. The Mercedes was still there.

"Guys, I can't outrun a Mercedes S- Class in a Beetle," I said.

"Who cares, drive motherfucker!" screamed Sam in between her laughter.

We shot out of the Haight Street intersection going the wrong way on Market. I hit the brake weaved in and out of the traffic. I saw the lights flash as soon as I heard the radio in my jacket pocket crackle to life.

"Shit, the cops," I said. "Maybe this will scare them off."

"Not my brothers!" said Charlie. "Drive!"

"Shit," said Lloyd, "Don't they care about the cops?"

"Not really," said Charlie. "They have them paid off."

I swung the Beetle into Gough Street across three lanes of traffic, and now I led a procession that consisted of a Beetle, a Mercedes and a police cruiser Crown Victoria. It was probably the lowest speed high-speed chase in San Francisco history. Not only this, but my scant advantage of apathy was erased by the fact that now cars were getting out of the way for the police siren. It could be argued that this helped us, but I didn't really expect to outrun radio or police cruiser in a Beetle. I wondered where all the radio traffic about this was when I had that thought, but I didn't have time to check my scanner at the moment.

I aimed the Beetle onto Division Street underneath the freeway. Now that two lanes were available, the police cruiser was trying to get around the Mercedes and failing. I saw the cruiser back off, and close in for a different maneuver.

Most police cars have huge rubber and steel bumpers. This bumper is specially designed for a move the police sometimes use to stop cars if there is no danger of hitting anything else – they will ram the rear bumper of the car they are chasing and use the massive police cruiser engine to push the car and destabilize the rear end of the fleeing vehicle. The cop was trying to do this to the Mercedes, and not having a good time of it. It gave the Mercedes driver the bright idea to try it on our piece of VW artwork.

I stared at the closing bumper in the window and searched desperately for a solution to this dilemma. Sam was cackling and Lloyd was yelling and Charlie seemed to have just disappeared – he wasn't making any noise. I yanked a hard right that made us skid onto Bryant Street as the cops and the Mercedes careened into each other while trying to turn and follow me.

I aimed the car at an alley next to a Hostess Twinkie factory on Bryant. The smell of chemical laden sponge cake permeated the air. We ran the car up into a small employees parking niche that was way out of view, and stopped the car. We got out and put as many feet between the car and us as possible.

We stopped in a shopping mall that was adjacent to the Hostess factory. The parking lot was nearly empty of cars and underground, so we paused here and tried to regroup before going up to catch the Fillmore bus back to our neighborhood.

"Well, we got rid of the car," said Lloyd.

"John's gonna kill us," I said.

"We'll deal with it," said Sam. "Just not now. We'll report it stolen."

"Why'd my brothers show up for me?" asked Charlie of nobody in particular.

We all turned to look at him.

###

"I honestly can't think of a reason," said Charlie. "They told me a long time ago they'd stay away from me."

"Why?" asked Sam.

"Because I don't like them," said Charlie. "They were always messed up in gangs, and never once did they regret what they did. They are criminals, and they stole everything they have."

"Wow, that's judgmental," said Lloyd. "Did they steal that Mercedes ?"

"No, they paid for it with money they made from their enterprises," said Charlie.

"So what do you think of my job?" asked Sam.

"What do you do?" asked Charlie. "We never talked about it."

Sam rolled her eyes.

"I jack off on the Internet for guys," she said.

Charlie got a surprised look on his face.

"You're still not exploiting other people to do what you do," he said.

"Well, I'm exploiting their need for sex," she said.

We were standing at the corner of Haight and Broderick after walking the steep hill up from the bus stop. I dreaded turning the corner, as I was certain Charlie's brothers would be waiting at the house.

"They are weak," said Charlie.

"When was the last time you got laid, Charlie?" asked Lloyd.

"None of your business," said Charlie.

We turned the corner, and there was nobody waiting. We walked the rest of the way to the house, past apartment buildings and small Victorian row houses. There was nobody waiting for us on our street either.

The door was not off its hinges and nothing in the house was disturbed, but there was a note with the mail.

"Some woman across the street is watching the house." said the note, and our landlord's scrawl signed it. Lloyd found the note.

"Great," he said. "They're watching us."

"Who are they?" I asked.

"Who cares?" asked Lloyd. "It's always 'they' anyway. Us and them."

I moved aside a curtain and saw a distinctive American made black automobile sitting across the street. A young woman sat in the car, and when observed directly appeared to be studiously avoiding looking at our house.

"I'll be back," I said, reflecting that direct confrontation seemed to work best in most situations when people were watching you.

I bounced down the stairs towards the street, and when I hit the curb I sprinted across to the unmarked car. The woman inside nearly freaked out when I opened the door and sat in the passenger seat.

"What the fuck!" she yelled.

"Calm down," I said.

"My partner is coming back in a second!" she yelled again, and started fumbling in her coat. I assessed the situation quickly.

She wasn't very large. I looked her up and down quickly. She was dressed a lot like I would imagine a secretary would be, except her clothing screamed "government employee": a knee length black skirt, white shirt, black jacket and black tie. I figured I might be able to overpower her in a fight – she looked to be a tiny bit over five and a half feet and maybe weighed a hundred or so pounds. I couldn't see her passing the FBI training program, but looks were often deceiving. I was basically staring at a female version of the notorious Man in Black. She was rather attractive as well, sporting icy blue eyes behind the glasses she was appraising me through. Her brown hair was pulled into tight bun, and I wondered what it might look like free – until I realized she was fumbling for a gun. I decided the best thing would be to let her pull it on me.

"Do you feel better?" I asked.

"What?" she asked.

"Do you feel better with the gun pointed at me?" I said.

"What kind of a question is that?" she asked.

"I'm just out here to talk to you," I said.

"What?" she asked.

"Oh come on, you've got our house under surveillance," I said.

She seemed to relax a little, but kept the gun pointed at me.

"I wasn't expecting you to walk out here and just sit in my car," she said.

"I know, most people don't," I said. "That's exactly why I do it."

"What do you want?" she demanded.

"Well, I'd like you to point that gun somewhere else for starters," I said.

The gun came down.

"Okay, now what?" she asked.

"Why are you watching our house?" I asked. "I mean, what reason? I can give you a few good ones, you know."

"What?" she asked.

"I'm not admitting guilt or anything, but there are some seriously weird things going on in that house," I said.

"You don't say?" she asked.

"Well, are you here for the black market in human body parts?" I asked.

"What?" she exclaimed.

"That's already gone, the evidence left when you arrested John." I said.

"Um, no," she said.

"Then why?" I asked. "Have you finally caught the landlord at something?"

"What?"

"Never mind," I said. "You sure do say 'what?' a lot."

"Look, I was just told to watch this house," she started. "My partner and I are with the local FBI…"

"Oh cool, like on TV?" I asked.

"No," she said icily, "Not like on TV."

"So why are you watching our house?" I asked.

"Look, I was ordered to," she said.

"Yeah, well, one of us has Chinese gang members out for him, does it have anything to do with that?" I asked.

"Listen, damn it," she said. "I'm just a field agent. I do what I'm told. I can't help you."

"You and everyone else," I said. "Why are you watching our house? Why can't you go catch those people that stole the neutron bomb?"

Her face paled visibly when I mentioned the neutron bomb, and the sudden flash of recognition gave her away.

"The neutron bomb? Around here?" I exclaimed.

"Shut up about it," she growled while looking around. "We thought you might know something since the gang that stole it visited you today."

"Charlie's brothers stole the neutron bomb?" I exclaimed.

"I'm not even supposed to tell you that!" she said.

"Then why are you?" I asked.

She blushed.

"It doesn't matter," she said, and then she looked at me. "But you should probably leave the city as soon as possible."

"Wow, you really are scared, aren't you?" I asked.

"Yeah, I am," she said. "I know what's going down."

"Finally, some answers," I said. "What about the pentagram?"

"Um, what?" she asked.

"Never mind," I said. "What do you know?"

###

I learned about the theft of the neutron bomb by Charlie's brothers as part of a large gang operation in Livermore. The lax security at the lab had allowed them to remove an assembled neutron bomb core – the only thing that they lacked was a timer. The thing was about the size of a softball – new technology was in place that allowed them to make the bomb this small. What she revealed to me left me shaking, sweating, and made me wonder whether or not to tell the others. None of it had to do with pentagrams.

199

30

Mission Dolores

I sat in the small graveyard looking at the small vial of ashes I usually wore on a chain around my neck.

There are only two graveyards in San Francisco. Three, technically, but one of them is a pet cemetery. I reflected upon this while looking at the vial of Cathy's ashes, and my mind suddenly thought about balance. Most places had graveyards and hospitals, but San Francisco only had two places for the dead. Of course, there were a lot of funeral homes nonetheless.

One of these graveyards is a military one, in the Presidio. The one I was currently sitting in was on the other side of town in the Mission.. I looked around me at the Mission Dolores graveyard and found myself happy for the privacy – a thick wall covered in ivy surrounds the place, and you can forget that the outside world even exists. Until the tourists get there, that is. Mission Dolores Church was once a Spanish mission in the 1700's, meaning that the graves are some of the oldest in San Francisco. They hold the first inhabitants of the city.

With only these two cemeteries, it seemed like the balance of San Francisco had been tipped too far into the scales of the living.

"You coming?" asked Sam as she peeked around the gate.

"Yes, I'll be there in a second," I said. "I'm just regaining my composure."

My composure was suffering because we passed a woman with glasses like cat eyes on the street.We were walking towards the statue in Mission

Dolores Park when I saw her coming towards us, and Sam grabbed my hand as I went after her.

"I know what I want," I said to the vial in my hand.

Cathy's ashes sat in my hand, looking at nothing in particular. I saw nothing there to connect with her image, or her personality. I wanted desperately to hear her laugh again. I wanted to hold her in my arms again. I wanted to live out my days with her.

I wasn't sure, but I think I had an answer.

I slipped Cathy's ashes back into my shirt , and stood up. The gate opened slightly, and as I pulled the heavy iron towards me I knew that what I had planned would work.

"Please watch over us," I said to the city fathers as I walked out of their graveyard. "We kind of need it right now."

\###

I looked at my watch nervously. We were on the way to the statue that formed the southeast corner of the pentacle I had plotted across the face of the city, and I knew that sometime I had to tell my friends the information I'd gotten while talking to the FBI agent. I figured that the best place to tell them would be at the statue.

"Why are we going out here again?" asked Lloyd. "Man, we measured this statue right after that Seth kid offed himself."

"I just want to be sure about how far it moved." I said.

"What does it matter?" asked Charlie. "I hope we don't run into my brothers again."

"Don't worry about that," I said."Did you notice that there's nobody out tonight?"

"Yeah," said Sam. "This is odd."

"I think that they all know," I said.

"Know what?" asked Sam.

"That they're all about to die." I said.

Everyone stopped.

"What?" asked Lloyd.

I looked up the street.We'd come to the corner of 19th and Dolores. There were a few apartment houses that had been built in the teens or twenties across the street, and we looked up into the center of Mission Dolores Park. A flower garden sat at the foot of the hill, and a statue of a man with his hand upraised looked down at those that walked up the fifty yards strips of pavement that shot towards the crown of the hill like a pair of crossbow bolts. I turned and looked at my companions.

"Well, if I'm wrong, we're all going to die." I said. "I would like to explain more a little closer to the statue."

Charlie, Sam, and Lloyd all regarded me dubiously. I could see that each of them thought I was a complete and total lunatic.

"I'll tell you on the way, then," I said. "We just have to get to that statue in less than ten minutes."

"Why ten minutes," asked Sam. "Why not twenty?"

"Well, let's talk on the way," I said, starting on the path. "We must maintain a sense of urgency!"

The others hurried around a planter and Sam grabbed my arm.

"Come on, sit here," she said, indicating a wall nearby. "I'm kind of worried about you."

I pulled my arm away and headed for the statue, less than a minute's walk away. We had plenty of time, I just wanted to explain to them while we were next to what I figured would be the protection of whatever spell there was over the city.

"The agent told me last night!" I said. "Come on, you guys!"

They all looked at me, confused as hell. After considering it a moment, they all scurried up the hill after me.

I had gotten to within thirty feet of the statue when I realized that there were already people there. I stopped, and as I waited for the rest of my friends to catch up, one of them noticed me.

It was a group of about ten people. They were all dressed in long black robes. They all seemed to be anywhere from forty to seventy. They were in a circle around the statue, and their presence only strengthened my conviction that I was on the right track.

"Hey, we're trying to do something here," said the one who noticed me.

"Yeah, I know," I said.

Lloyd came up behind me at that point, as I pulled the backpack off of my back.

"What's up?" asked Sam, coming up to my right.

One of the people in robes broke off and moved towards us as Charlie got to us.

"We'd really appreciate it if you could come back in about fifteen minutes," smiled the older man at us.

Everyone looked at me.

"Sorry, I came up here looking for you," I said. "Besides, we've only got about ten minutes left."

All the people in robes turned their heads to look at me.

"Oh my," said the older man closest to us. "This is unexpected."

I pulled the book out of my backpack. A slight gasp rose from the circle.

"Derwood," growled Lloyd, "Who are these people?"

"You mean you don't know any of these Satanists?" I asked.

Another gasp went up from the circle.

"See here," said one of the circle. "We're all…"

Another gasp went up as I pulled out the Hand of Glory.

"Lloyd, do you remember what I told you about the parameters of the spell being defined by the rumors being said about it?" I asked.

"Yeah," he said. The old guy moved away from us, and several other men and a woman dressed in black robes broke away from the circle and moved towards us.

"Well, what have we figured out powers this spell?" I asked.

"Death," said Sam and Lloyd simultaneously.

Charlie suddenly started to understand, and he slowly moved to intercept the people advancing on us.

"Right," I said. "So, guess what the FBI agent told me?"

Sam started to shake.

"Oh jeez," said Lloyd. "You stupid shit."

"What?" I asked.

"You're going to get us killed!" Lloyd snarled. "She told you that neutron bomb was going to go off in about ten minutes!"

"Seven," I said, looking at my watch.

"Oh god," said Sam. "Oh god, this is it."

"Get rid of them," barked the older man.

One of them swung at Charlie, who easily sidestepped him.

The second one pulled out a long black stick, and Charlie took it from him and started hitting all the men.

"So why are these guys fighting Charlie?" I asked Lloyd.

"What?" he asked.

"Think, Satan Boy," I said. "These guys seemed to know what I was talking about. The FBI agent told me unknown parties purchased it but it was rumored that Satanists were behind it. They were watching us because of Charlie's brothers, but they had you on file as a Satanist."

"I'm on file as a Satanist with the FBI?" asked Lloyd.

"Hold that ego down, boy," I said. "We're not done yet."

I took out a lighter and held the Hand of Glory out.

"We have to light this, and then we can do what these guys were going to do," I said. "At this point, it's our only hope for survival."

As Charlie smacked five men on the forehead with the stick in rapid succession, the female robed person tried to punch him. This clearly troubled Charlie.

Sam stopped shaking and looked at me.

"What the fuck? What the hell were they going to do?" asked Sam.

"What would you do if you had the biggest spell in the world at your disposal?" I asked. "They were all going to be granted one wish."

I lit one of the fingers on the hand, and Lloyd put his hand in mine.

"Make a chain, Sam," instructed Lloyd.

What happened next was almost a complete blur. Charlie and the raging battle he was waging next to us got a little out of hand. Three of the men had grabbed onto Charlie's clothes, and he was flinging them around as they tried to hang on. Using a free hand, he smacked one of them in the face with a sickening crunch, and the other two let go. One of them flew between Sam and Lloyd about a foot before their hands touched.

"Ouch," said Lloyd.

I lit another finger.

"Charlie, when I say go, come grab Sam's hand!" shouted Lloyd.

Charlie used the stick he'd stolen on several groins before the woman ran up to him again. Charlie ducked, and one of her male companions punched her in the face. She went down hard on her ass, but she shook her head and started to stand up again.

"OK!" said Charlie. He looked like he was having fun.

I lit a third finger.

"What do we wish for?" asked Sam.

"I don't care," I said. "I know what I'm going to wish for."

"What?" asked Sam.

"You know, I don't have much of a family," I said. "I regard all of you as my family. Cathy and my child are part of my family. I just want my family to be alive and well and living in San Francisco."

Lloyd and Sam regarded me.

"We're a family," said Sam. "I like that. I can go with that."

"Hey, if it saves my ass, I'll do anything," said Lloyd.

I lit the fourth finger.

"We have two minutes left," I said.

"OK," said Lloyd. "I'm going to call to Charlie, and when he touches Sam, you light that thumb."

"OK," I said, lighter at the ready.

"Charlie!" shouted Lloyd. "Time's up!"

I watched as Charlie punched three men off of him and sprinted at Sam.

Halfway across the grass, the woman who has taken so much damage at the hands of her fellow robed ones leaned in and managed to snag Charlie's foot. He tripped, and as he flew forward I saw one of the neatest feats of acrobatics I'd ever seen – Charlie hit the grass on his hands, did a complete double handspring, and landed on his feet next to Sam after turning twice in the air.

"I always try to do things in twos," he said as he grabbed Sam's hand.

I held the lighter to the thumb, and as it caught the world grew very silent. "Whoa," I said.

All around us, the robed people fell away in a trancelike state. The older man had hung back near the statue, and we moved as a group towards the statue.

"OK, Charlie," said Sam. "When the light flashes, we get one wish. So wish for your family to be happy and healthy and living in San Francisco."

"That's easy," said Charlie. "That's what I wish for every day anyway."

We managed to stretch around the base of the statue, one of us to each side of the base. The Hand of Glory helped a little bit – we used it as kind of an extender by holding on to the ends of the piece of wood. I checked my watch and then grabbed Charlie's hand.

"OK," I said. "Any second now."

I closed my eyes and wished for my family to be safe, sound, happy and whole and alive in San Francisco as a flash burned my eyelids and nuclear light filled the skin. I felt the hot sleet of charged neutrons smash my nervous system, as they disrupted the impulses in every nerve. The electricity that drove my body ceased to flow. At that instant, I died.

31

The End

The neutron bomb had gone off on the rickety Sutro Tower. A ball of plasma about one thousand feet in diameter had vaporized the giant antenna, and bathed the entire city of San Francisco with neutron radiation. Every single person in the city had collapsed in a dead, twitching heap almost instantly. I figured that whoever set it was trying to get it high enough to cover the city while avoiding the destruction of any really nice houses.

We all died. We're pretty sure of that. The instant in which we died in seemed to last for a lifetime. Lloyd, Sam, Charlie and I talked about it later.

We all saw the demon, and then we were back in what we think is the real world.

My theory is that we saw TUTIVILLUS, and he set things to the way we wished them to be. Lloyd tends to agree. Charlie and Sam are still debating it. Cathy doesn't care.

When I opened my eyes, I was holding Cathy's hand. That was fine by me – it's all I wanted. I don't ask any questions about that.

I can't begin to express the joy that overtook me. I thought I would never be able to kiss her lips again. The vial of ash around my neck was gone, and Cathy never felt more real or felt so good. I held her with tears streaming out of my eyes while the others looked away. I was incoherent for a while, until Cathy spoke.

"Why are there bodies everywhere?" she asked.

It was true. We looked around at the city, and everywhere we turned were bodies.

We broke into an apartment flat across the street from the park. A body, covered in what looked like bad sunburn, was lying in the stairwell leading up to the door.

We went to the Safeway at Church and Market – various hipsters had croaked in the middle of buying dinner to cook. We wandered the aisles, taking shopping cart after shopping cart of food. When it was all over, we found a dead dot com millionaire lying in the magazine aisle, and with his car alarm key chain we found his SUV in the parking lot. The large vehicle chirped at us from across the lot when we pushed the remote control buttons.

The landlord died in the neutron blast. We found him when we got back to the house. He'd been torturing someone when the blast went off – thankfully, it probably helped the poor victim. Body parts were still stacked like cordwood in his apartment, and the stench of formaldehyde meant that he probably would have died of cancer if it hadn't been for this.

"Good riddance," said Lloyd.

San Francisco was going to get extremely stinky in a few days, and we didn't know what to do about that. We all agreed that we should probably leave. In the middle of this discussion, Cathy ran to the bathroom and vomited up the toaster pastries she'd pilfered from Safeway. I nearly cried again when I realized she was still pregnant – it was as if she'd never died. I wanted to stay in San Francisco, but I had to face the facts that if we stayed that there would be no doctors to help deliver the baby, and we'd be living in a huge, disease ridden pile of corpses.

"Hey, man," said Lloyd. "I have a question."

"Shoot," I said.

"We found a bunch of robed weirdoes around that statue," he said. "What about all the other statues?"

"What do you mean?" asked Sam.

"If there were robed weirdoes around our statue," I said, "then there must have been robed weirdoes around at least the other four statues in the outer edge of the pentagram."

"Oh shit," said Sam.

"Yeah," said Lloyd. "And what do you think they wished for?"

We found a trash dumpster outside the corner café, and we wheeled it up to the landlord's apartment door. We cleaned all the body parts out of the basement apartment, and we gently placed the landlord's body on top of the arms in the dumpster. We moved the dumpster across the street and prepared to burn it the next day. I figured the smoke would attract some kind of rescue craft. We never got around to burning the body parts, unfortunately.

That night, we sat on the roof and watched the fires burning Nob Hill and Pacific Heights to the ground.

###

Sam noticed it first. She was standing in the front window when a person walked by, about four or five days later.

"Hey!" she screamed out the front window.

The person lumbered to a stop. She thought he was dazed or in shock at first – his ashen face seemed to have no emotion to it.

As she opened the front door, the person looked up and Sam saw that he had no eyeballs.

She slammed to door shut and ran back to the window.

The person tripped on the stairs, and as he repeatedly fell against the pavement, Sam noticed odd things. One of his arms was broken. Large portions of his skin were rotting. He kept moaning incoherently. The kicker was the fact that as she watched him, the landlord crawled out of the dumpster and tried to join him.

The landlord had three human arms grabbing him in various places, holding on for dear unlife.

Sam did what nearly all of us wanted to do when we found out – she screamed bloody murder. We sat at the front window trying to plot our next move.

"Why is this happening?" asked Cathy.

"You're alive," I said. "I wished you back from the dead."

"Yes, I know," said Cathy impatiently. "But who wished for zombies?"

"Not me," said Charlie.

"Not me," said Lloyd.

"Not me," I said.

We all looked at Sam.

"OK, I cheated a bit," she said sheepishly.

"What did you wish for?" I demanded.

"Um," she started, "I wished for my family to be happy and whole. You people are my family."

"Is that it?" I asked.

"No," she said, lowering her eyes. "I wished for my family to be happy and whole and the only living people in San Francisco."

"Shit!" said Lloyd. "Not when dealing with the demon in charge of nit-picking! We are so fucked now!"

"Calm down," I said to Lloyd. "It just means that we can't leave for a while."

"Try forever," he said. "Do you know how many corpses are in this city?"

"Well, no." I said. "I don't. I think we need to think about finding a more secure place to live."

###

That's how we come to our present situation. It's been about a year since the neutron blast. San Francisco is a haven for the walking dead. When the neutron blast happened and the zombies started roaming, the government decided the only way to solve the problem was to blow the bridges and build a wall across the peninsula. San Francisco was left to the zombies. Well, it was left to the zombies and us.

We've learned how to live with zombies. Most of them are really rotten by now – they aren't much of a problem anymore. One good hit with a baseball bat to the head is enough to knock the all-important head off, but the bodies still twitch even if they have no head. It only took one corpse grabbing my ankle to make a machete standard issue for roaming the streets.

We moved to the paramilitary home of Wanda the Satanist on California Street. It already had the half-inch steel plates covering all the windows, and for some reason was completely locked and devoid of zombies.

Lloyd has lost weight, and has really gotten into guns. They had a huge stash of guns in the Satanic Clubhouse.

Charlie keeps thinking he sees his brothers wandering around San Francisco.

Sam has cheered up immensely. I think this is due to the fact that the city is a lot less crowded nowadays.

Cathy and I are making a go of raising our child in San Francisco. It turned out that the lack of doctors didn't really matter much – people have been giving birth for thousands of years without doctors, and Sam and I managed to help deliver the baby without much trouble. I tried not to think about the zombies pounding on the steel reinforced front door – I swear, those things can smell blood through ten feet of concrete.

Some days I feel like I'm not even alive. I feel like a ghost wandering the ruined hulk of my beloved city, doomed forever to torment and fear – fear of zombies and of living in the hellish place San Francisco has become. I don't care much, though – I have Cathy, and our kid, and life really seems to be worth living. Even if Lloyd, Charlie, Sam and I all died that day when the neutron bomb went off, I'm still content with everything. I'm not in hell – I have Cathy and that is nothing like hell. It's more like I'm a ghost – a ghost raising a child with my wife and chosen family.

San Francisco is a great place to raise a kid, except for all the damned zombies.

THE END

About the Author

Darren Mckeeman originally hails from Atlanta, Georgia but his home is San Francisco since 1996. His teenage brushes with the law for computer hacking gave him time to win a contest for writing in jail, and he's written a lot of things since then - newspaper articles, novels, tabletop game manuals, business plans, and many, many tweets. He spends his time restoring and sailing an old sailboat.

Subscribe to my newsletter:
✉ https://linktr.ee/tjcrowley

Also by Darren Paul Mckeeman

Darren writes mostly fiction and essays.

America's Last Emperor

Joshua Abraham Norton is an immigrant with a secret. He comes to San Francisco during the 1849 Gold Rush to set himself up in business, but finds himself swept up in dramatic events unfolding all around him with little to no way of controlling what happens to him or the people that he considers friends. San Francisco History unfolds before his eyes, even as his own story prepares to overshadow the entire story of San Francisco for the next twenty years.